THE TRAP

An absolutely gripping crime mystery with a massive twist

MICHAEL LEESE

Martha Munro Crime Mysteries Book 2

Joffe Books, London
www.joffebooks.com

First published in Great Britain in 2023

Cover art by Nick Castle

ISBN: 978-1-80405-997-5

PROLOGUE

Present day

"Get up, bitch. It's time you died."

The woman spat the words at her target, then instantly regretted her loss of control.

Looking down at the victim splayed across the bed, she feared she'd been too heavy-handed when she'd dosed her vodka.

The killer tried a different approach.

"Your garden looks amazing. Don't you want to see it?"

The words, spoken in a honeyed tone, almost stuck in her throat. But after a moment they started to work. The woman staggered up, her expression dreamy as she lurched across the room.

The killer followed, licking her lips in anticipation of what was to come. This was her chance to prove she could handle cold-blooded murder.

It was a carefully planned killing that called for a cool head and nerves of steel.

Now she had the target where she wanted her.

"Why don't you lean out of the window and smell the flowers?" she urged, her teeth bared in excitement. "A little closer, you're almost there."

Finally, the victim was in place.

She flexed her fingers and placed her hands on her buttocks, marvelling at how bony they were.

"Bye-bye, loser," she said out loud as she shoved hard. The woman slipped headfirst through the window, and for the briefest of moments there was silence, followed by a faint crunching sound.

* * *

Nine months earlier

Audrey Taylor was so angry her voice was shrill. "We've been betrayed, my darling, betrayed . . . I was warned this would happen!"

Imelda glanced curiously at her mother. She wondered who could have issued this warning. As far as she knew, Audrey had no friends. She was a woman who kept her secrets carefully locked away. But over the last few months her mother had become ever more volatile, a response to the sudden deterioration in her health that had seen her body swell beyond recognition.

Was it her illness, which the doctors claimed they could do nothing about, driving this notion of betrayal? Surely it was far too dramatic an interpretation of her failure to secure an interview for a job in publishing, an exercise to which Imelda had reluctantly applied herself after feigning an interest in the literary world in order to pacify her mother. Audrey saw her attainment of a 2:2 in English literature as a stepping stone to great things. Imelda, though, was rather more realistic about the true value of such a middling degree. But at twenty-two years old she also knew it was easiest to follow Mother's orders.

A few weeks earlier, Audrey had amazed her daughter by coming up with some 'suggestions' about which publishers to approach. Given that she had never seen her mother read anything bar a tabloid newspaper, it was a big surprise. With a shrug, Imelda cobbled together a list topped with her mother's ideas. Doing anything else would have triggered a sulk, :and she was anxious to avoid that: every time Audrey got angry it seemed to Imelda that her health nudged downwards.

Imelda knew the slow response from the publishers hadn't helped. It took several weeks for the first 'don't call us' reply to land via email. It was another fortnight before the second rejection arrived. Audrey had pursed her lips but said nothing.

It was the fifth response, deep into the second month since she'd sent out her applications, that triggered the outburst. It had come from one of her mother's suggested publishers and brought matters to a head as they sipped pre-dinner drinks while sitting side by side in battered, mismatched recliners positioned in front of an oversized TV balanced on a cheap pine chest of drawers. After changing into her evening outfit — a tent-like gown that was one of the few items of clothing she didn't threaten to burst out of — Audrey insisted on a very large measure of sweet sherry before eating. This time she was on her second 'snifter' and watched intently as Imelda opened the message on her iPad. She read it and then passed it to her mother, who was making grabbing motions with her left hand, the other meaty fist wrapped around her glass of sherry.

They were in the cramped but clean front room of a council flat above a shop close to Brixton High Street. Audrey, who was now seriously bloated, was finding the stairs increasingly hard work and had started making loud wheezing noises as she dragged her body up the two short flights before making it through the front door and collapsing into her armchair.

Imelda urged her to see the doctor again, but her mother had rejected her plea, complaining that on her last visit, which had taken weeks to arrange, she had been told her condition was caused by a heart problem for which nothing could be done. Imelda doubted this was the whole story, but also understood that her mother had a phobia of doctors at the best of times and tried to ignore all medical issues in the hope they would melt away. It left Imelda frantic with worry, but quite unable to persuade her mother to try something different. She suggested a trip to A&E, but this was dismissed out of hand.

With health forcing retirement from her cleaning jobs, Audrey used what little energy she had to work on the two-bedroomed flat twice a day: first thing in the morning and again in the late afternoon, the final polish completed at precisely 4.30 p.m. Then it was sherry time.

She'd already started on the drink as she studied the message from a publishing house so grand Imelda would never have selected it. Her mother's lips moved as she slowly read the rejection. Finally, she took it all on board and the result was fascinating. She went very red, then purple, repeating the words '*no vacancies at this time*' over and over. Sweat beaded on her brow and she seemed to forget about breathing as she gasped and gurgled before regaining some semblance of control, although the drool escaping from the corner of her mouth did not inspire confidence. She gulped her remaining sherry in one go, then looked at her daughter with an intensity that thrilled and scared her in equal measure.

"You know what this is," said Audrey, waving the tablet around. "It's proof." She went very still and closed her eyes, apparently lost in thought. Imelda was still marvelling at how purple her mother had become when the eyes snapped open.

"Get me another drink," she commanded. "And make it large. I need to think."

Imelda managed to fit half a bottle into one of their bigger glasses and passed it to her mother, who quickly downed it.

"Another!"

Imelda leaped to do her bidding. Mummy had never drunk more than two glasses before, but now she was on the second bottle. The drink went down and then Audrey closed her eyes again. *What could she be thinking?* wondered Imelda. At which point Audrey started snoring, very loudly. Ten minutes later she snorted and opened her eyes, which locked on to Imelda.

"There's a lot I need to tell you before we can have our revenge. But it will be ours. They can pay in blood for what they've done."

Imelda was thrilled. As her fears for her mother had grown, so had the intensity of her dreams. Recently she'd been dreaming of blood, powerful visions that left her gasping for more. Maybe her wishes were about to come true.

CHAPTER 1

Martha Munro failed to suppress the shudder which threatened to emerge the moment Detective Sergeant Roger Edwards slithered uncomfortably close to the outer edge of her personal space. She thought he was repulsive at the best of times; standing this close made her flesh crawl. There was a creepy quality to the man, and more than once she'd caught him leering at her.

Right now, he was standing at her desk presenting a thin file and a broad grin, his dirty grey teeth like tiny tombstones. It wasn't a friendly grin; one look at his piggy eyes told her that. They were sparkling with malicious glee, and the smell of his cheap aftershave combined with his BO to nauseous effect.

In a perfect world she would have ignored him — even better walked away — but he effectively ran the detective roster at Croydon police station, assigning officers as cases came in. It granted him a degree of power not matched by his talent.

She gingerly accepted the file that he thrust at her. It contained a single sheet of paper and didn't take her long to read. She kept a neutral expression as she imagined tossing the file into the rubbish bin.

"I thought it would be suitable for your abilities and experience," said Sergeant Edwards. "And Dulwich is your neck of the woods, so you won't have far to travel."

"You want me to leave the office and investigate this?" Martha was proud that her voice betrayed nothing of the anger she was feeling.

"You're a quick one, for sure," he said, grinning again like an evil imp.

"Can I point out that cats go missing all the time," said Martha. "Just for the record — all these cats went missing and came back. Surely this can be left with the local beat team. Isn't this exactly what we have community officers for?"

A sly expression crossed his face. It was a clue that he'd been thinking, not something he was known for.

"Ah, well," he said, rubbing his hands together. "That's the point, ain't it?"

Martha waited. Silently.

"It's like the new commissioner said last week: she wants to see more attention paid to the everyday stuff. The idea is we sweat the small things and that improves the big picture. It could be cats today, cocaine tomorrow."

Preoccupied with his own cleverness, he missed her contemptuous shake of the head at this dim-witted analysis. She headed off any further comment by getting to her feet. For a moment they stood close together, and Martha was pleased to see him flinch. He was short and going to seed, she was tall and athletic . . . no doubting the outcome if push came to shove.

"I'm going to get a sandwich from the canteen. When I get back, I'll get right onto the cats," said Martha as she walked away.

"I knew you'd be right for the pussies," he called out before sniggering.

Martha resisted the urge to grab him and toss him out of the second floor window.

By the time she returned she was calm enough to be philosophical. Of course, this cat mystery was a deliberate wind-up, but she was going to have to put up with it, for now.

She reminded herself that while this was painfully dull, it was better than being in prison, where she had been not that long ago. The victim of a conspiracy orchestrated, in part, by a very senior Scotland Yard officer. It had claimed her mother's life and resulted in the abduction of her five-year-old daughter, Betty.

A subsequent investigation proved beyond doubt she was an innocent victim, but that wasn't the end of the power games. If there was anything guaranteed to make the top brass anxious it was the suggestion of senior-level corruption. It was one thing to have an ordinary detective accepting bags of cash, quite another for one of the Met's officer class to be caught orchestrating a conspiracy aimed at an innocent junior officer. Once the facts became known, the commissioner made it clear it was to be kept under wraps. The suits proposed a deal, one that no one could talk about. Martha agreed on the condition that she was allowed to return to her life as a newly minted detective based at Croydon police station. At twenty-five years old she was one of the Met's youngest detectives, and there was talk she was set to follow in the illustrious footsteps of her father, a decorated officer known as a fierce scourge of corrupt coppers.

Even so, she needed to keep her head down. There were those in the force who liked to say, "There's no smoke without fire." It was whispered that perhaps the 'Golden Girl' wasn't so golden after all, and in an organisation the size of the Met there was plenty of room for malicious rumours to flourish. What better than the suggestion that the daughter of a decorated senior officer might be mixed up in wrongdoing? That there was not a shred of evidence to support this idea didn't get a look-in. She had learned the hard way that for all its good qualities, the Met could be a savage place for the unwary.

CHAPTER 2

Martha took a deep breath and got to work. She would do this by the book, resisting the urge to cut corners. If Sergeant Edwards wanted a full-on investigation, then a full-on investigation was what he was going to get. She'd already established that a chief inspector, Tony Green, was the officer leading the Safer Neighbourhood Team covering the Dulwich area and left a message on his phone.

Not wanting to hang around, she grabbed a pool car and headed for Dulwich. She should have gone through Edwards for the vehicle, but the small act of defiance made her feel better. He could hardly complain having talked up the importance of the job. Once on the road she decided to head into the heart of the village and wear out some shoe leather to see if there was anything to be gained from studying the geography of the incidents. Just being on the move helped Martha cool down. A rueful smile crossed her lips as she contemplated the 'Moggie Mystery' . . . not one to garland her CV.

She had six addresses where a cat had been reported missing, the locations all within walking distance, and a couple very close to each other. Despite living in West Dulwich, she rarely came into the centre of the village. It wasn't an area she knew well, other than it boasted some of the more expensive property and among the businesses was a children's shoe shop where she took her daughter Betty for school shoes.

Her rumbling stomach reminded her she was hungry. The ham sandwich she'd bought in the canteen had been stale and dry, and she'd thrown it away after one bite. Not wanting to risk her tummy gurgling while she was on the doorstep, she spotted a deli near the shoe shop and decided it was worth a go. She might as well talk to the staff and customers — they would know if the cats were the talk of the village.

Twenty minutes later she had a falafel wrap and not an iota of practical information. She had needed every ounce of her resolve as she met a wall of ridicule, even hostility. One man, who clearly fancied himself a comic, had responded to her questions with a long-winded and unfunny skit that compared her unflatteringly to Sherlock Holmes. A couple of others demonstrated anger that she was investigating such a trivial issue while 'real crimes' needed attention. Many police officers would have called it a day at that point — the cats were hardly the talk of the village and she had already gone above and beyond. But Martha wasn't a quitter, and running into difficulties only made her more determined. If there was something going on, she would find it. She ate her lunch and girded herself for the next thankless task . . . talking to the owners who had reported the incidents. She had a sinking feeling they would all be fanatical about their pets and demand a level of police effort that was out of step with what was merited. She was trying to generate some enthusiasm when her efforts were interrupted by a call from Chief Inspector Tony Green.

"Your message said you've been assigned to investigating the cats," said the officer. "I don't mean to be rude, but is this serious? I mean, does it really need a detective on the case?"

"Those are my orders," said Martha, sounding a bit sharp. Green's obvious amazement had hit a raw nerve. She gripped her phone and tried again. "As you say, sir, it does seem a bit over the top. But none the less, that's what I need to do. If I'm honest, the quicker I get this over with the better."

"In that case how can I help you, Detective Constable Munro?"

"I'd like to talk to whoever handled the initial inquiries, if that's possible?" said Martha, relieved that he was willing to play this with a straight bat.

"No problem. It was one of my community officers, PCSO Krisha Patel," he said. "She's quite new but a great officer who's going places. She'll be in a meeting I'm holding at Walworth Road police station in an hour. Just ask for the Dulwich Safer Neighbourhood session. You can talk to her and meet some of the rest of the team, if you like."

She could tell his offer was well intended — but she wished all this effort was directed towards something a bit more serious. She was all for being tough on small crimes, but she wasn't yet able to say that an actual crime had been committed.

CHAPTER 3

Walworth Road police station was never going to win any prizes for architecture. Constructed from dark yellow bricks, it had windows and doors the shade of which suggested the architect could have done with support when it came to colour matching. The overall effect did nothing to disguise the boxy appearance that was typical of so many police stations. The most flattering description was *functional*. Martha reported in and was quickly guided towards the room where Chief Inspector Green was holding his meeting. He was about Martha's height, physically fit and had an open face with light hazel eyes. He looked at her steadily as she entered the room.

"Detective Martha Munro, I presume," he said brightly, as Martha added good-looking and cheerful to the mental profile she had built up. She was relieved. Some officers in his position could sound like they'd just come from a training seminar. He was also efficient, swiftly guiding her towards Krisha Patel, who was standing at the back of the room and clearly waiting for her. Martha noted a woman in her late twenties who radiated the kind of calm and controlled energy which suggested she looked after herself. Krisha smiled warmly and Martha felt they would get on well.

To Martha's surprise, the chief inspector showed no sign of moving away. If anything, he looked anxious.

"I've got a confession to make," said Green, his face creasing in apology. "Maybe I've allowed this one to slip under the radar. If you don't mind, I'll stay involved, at least for the moment. I don't like having operations going on in my patch that I'm not familiar with. As far as I was concerned, we checked it at the time and there was nothing to it, so we rightly put it back in its box. Now DC Munro is here to take another look, so I'll listen in for a moment. Krish, perhaps you can take both me and DC Munro through this right from the moment you were first briefed about it?"

"OK, sir," said the PCSO, taking a moment to gather her thoughts. "It started when you asked me to call an Assistant Commissioner Heath Jones. It turned out he knew one of the families who were complaining about a cat, and he instructed me to make sure we looked into it."

The chief inspector looked at her with a rueful expression. "Of course. It came from so high up the food chain, I was worried you'd get a nosebleed."

Martha added a sense of humour to her mental profile.

Krisha smiled. "I spent four days on it but there wasn't much to show. I was amazed such a senior officer was taking an interest. Each story was the same. The cats went missing then returned. It seemed a lot of fuss about nothing, but the assistant commissioner demanded I report to a Sergeant Edwards, based in Croydon. He stressed I wasn't to bother you with it, that this Sergeant Edwards would do it all." Martha felt herself stiffen at the man's name but kept quiet as Krisha paused and looked at her boss. "Permission to speak off the record, sir?" Tony gave her a brief smile of encouragement and Krisha didn't pull her punches. "Sergeant Edwards is a strange man, in my opinion. He never seemed to know what was going on. I had to ring him twice one day, each time I needed to tell him who I was."

Her comment induced a snort from Martha. "Since we're having an off-the-record moment . . . I'm more than familiar with the man and, trust me, you're not alone in your opinion." She reached up and unconsciously pinched her earlobe. "I can see an inexperienced junior detective and a PCSO involved in this, but a sergeant is pushing it, and as for an assistant commissioner . . . It seems very odd."

To her surprise the chief inspector joined in. "I spent some time as a younger officer working under the direction of Sergeant Edwards. In my view he wasn't fit to be in charge of making the tea." He held up a hand. "Not that I would say that on the record."

Martha resisted the urge to cheer. "Getting back to cats — as we must — Krisha, did your investigation find anything? Did the owners know each other? Were they valuable cats? Any witnesses? Were the cats hurt in any way?"

Krisha kept shaking her head. "Nothing at all."

Martha frowned in frustration. "It sounds like a complete waste of time."

"That's exactly what I thought," said Krisha, "at first." This grabbed Martha's attention. "Sergeant Edwards didn't tell you about the text message?"

"What text message?" asked Tony.

"The assistant commissioner told me not to mention it to anyone. He told me Sergeant Edwards would assign a detective and I was to keep that information to myself. He said it was strictly 'need to know' and if it got out, he'd know who to blame." She took a breath. "Well, Martha is here now, which changes things. I don't need to keep it secret."

"What was the text message?" asked Martha. "Because I can assure you that our illustrious detective sergeant didn't mention it to me either."

Krisha didn't need to check her notes. "It was sent to the Brown family, about a week after their cat returned. It said: 'Next time it's the kids.' It terrified them."

She looked embarrassed. "I should have told you, sir," she said to Tony, "but Assistant Commissioner Jones really laid it on about not telling you and it was forcibly backed up by the sergeant."

The chief inspector waved the apology away. "This should never have happened." He noted the crestfallen expression on Krisha's face. "And no one is blaming you, Krish. You were given a direct order by a senior officer. But now we all know, so let's get on with it. I'll get to Sergeant Edwards in good time, but for now we need to chase up this text message." He glanced at Martha. "I think we both know why he chose you. He likes dumping what he thinks of as the rubbish on female officers."

Martha almost bridled at his bluntness but then shrugged it off. "I can't disagree with you, sir. But from my point of view, it's good news. He appears to have given me a proper case by mistake. Although I wonder why he didn't mention the text. Even he must have thought it makes the cats worth looking at again."

"I'm not surprised," said Tony. "From what I've heard, he'd forget his own name if it wasn't written on his warrant card. Like I said, leave him to me." He slowly rubbed his hands together. "Let's pretend we're starting at the beginning. I want you two to keep me fully informed. That especially includes anyone suggesting I don't need to know what's going on in my patch. If it was just threats against animals, I'd still take it seriously, but threats against children cross a line. Now, when did you hear about the text, Krish?"

"Two days ago, sir. I was told it was all in hand."

Tony rolled his eyes. "This is all wrong. You two get going and I'll talk to the divisional superintendent. I think we may need to offer protection to this family."

CHAPTER 4

Martha's eyes lit up as she outlined a plan of action. "We need to get going with the Browns. I can't believe we're already two days behind on this investigation and nothing's been done — although," she said, reaching out and lightly patting Krisha on her upper arm, "none of this is on you."

Over the last couple of hours, Krisha had looked energised by working with Martha, as if she wanted to show what she could do. She checked her notes. "Mr Brown is working from home and told us to come straight round."

"Grab your gear and let's go," said Martha. "I'll drive us down there and you can carry on ringing around. Find out if anyone else has been targeted."

Twenty minutes later and they were outside one of the more substantial houses in the centre of Dulwich Village. It was set back from the road, with a path leading to a set of steps and the front door of a four-storey property.

"I've always wondered what one of these places was like," said Martha.

"All the houses on this list are pretty amazing, but I couldn't even afford to keep the windows clean," Krisha replied, eyeing two men working a cherry picker as they set up to do the top floor windows.

"You and me both," laughed Martha. "Before we bang on the door, any thoughts on Mr Brown, and did you meet his wife?"

"No to the wife," replied Krisha. "Mr Brown was polite but a bit distant. He runs a hedge fund, whatever that means."

"It means he can afford to live here," said Martha. "Come on, then. Let's go. No point worrying about houses we can never buy."

As they walked up to the front door a youngish man with a wheelbarrow appeared. He was tall and wearing a T-shirt and shorts. Martha watched him disappear around the other side of the house and made a mental note that they were going to need a list of all the various staff who worked for the family, both in and out of the house. She wondered if the Browns employed someone whose duties included keeping tabs on everyone who was around.

At that moment a man answered the door. He was in his forties and looked like he was dressed for a day in the office rather than working from home. His shirt was crisp and white, with gold cufflinks. His tie was pink and knotted perfectly. The look was completed with black formal trousers and gleaming brogues. His thick, dark brown hair looked freshly trimmed. He was a couple of inches taller than Martha, and something about his manner said this was a man used to being in charge. His opening remarks removed any doubt.

"You took your time," he said, glaring at each of them in turn.

"I'm sorry you've had to wait for a follow-up on the text message," said Martha. "But I can assure you we're taking it seriously."

She was careful not to react to his terse greeting. Much as she hated starting with an apology, he did have a point. This had come close to being missed. Mr Charles Brown turned on his heel and walked back into the large entrance way. The pair took it as an invitation and followed him inside, Martha carefully closing the front door behind her as she watched him head to the left of the central staircase into what was obviously his home office. The room was dominated by a bank of screens on the wall opposite his desk which were displaying share prices as they happened with swathes of changing reds and blues showing how fast prices were moving.

The effect was hypnotic, and both officers watched the information flowing across the screens. Brown, who was used to the effect, languidly waved a hand. "That gives me the real-time financial information I need." He aimed his chin at the screens. "That's a lot of data. The local broadband isn't quite up to it, so I had a satellite system installed. It cost an arm and a leg, but I don't miss anything — and the wretched Zoom calls are crystal clear."

He gestured to a table in the corner. "Please sit down and help yourselves." There was a jug of coffee and bottles of water laid out.

Martha declined but her colleague gratefully took a drink. The detective waited until Krisha was ready before speaking.

"Would you mind going over everything from the start?" she asked.

As they sat down, Brown scratched the tip of his nose. "Potted history first . . . then the sinister bit?"

Martha nodded in approval.

"We moved here twelve months ago," said Brown. "My wife wanted more space. I run a hedge fund and, yes, I realise that mentioning hedge funds to most people is a red flag, but we're ethical investors and we pay all our taxes in the UK." He threw his hands wide. "So, there you have it, Charles Brown in a nutshell."

Martha was happy to keep the questions quite general for now. "Can you talk me through family members and all the different people who work for you?"

"There's my wife, Summer, son Tom, aged seven, and daughter Amelia, five. As to staff here at the house, that's my wife's arena, but I can get the details. The only other people here are my company's IT team, but they have all been subjected to deep background checks."

"Do you often have work meetings at home?" asked Martha.

"Not many," he said. "If I need to see people I travel to my office, near St Paul's Cathedral. I only work from home if there's no other way — like right now, when we've had threats."

"What about friends or enemies?" said Martha.

"I don't have many friends, if I'm honest," said Brown. "I know a lot of people, but I'm not one for socialising for the sake of it. As to enemies . . . did I mention I run a hedge fund?"

"Are you saying you've received threats before?" asked Martha, leaning forward in her seat.

"Over the years, yes. A great many," said Brown. "They follow the same pattern. We invest in some company, there's a lot of opposition from various vested interests, then death threats appear on social media. It's all a bit boring actually, but our security people keep an eye, just in case."

"You sound as though you're almost relaxed about it," said Martha.

"That's the way it goes. In a way it's like a badge of honour. My people do track down the odd idiot who's not good at disguising themselves. They discovered a serial threat maker was a little old lady in a care home, using the staff iPad. Had to admire the determination." What might have been a smile touched his lips, but it was a blink-and-miss-it moment.

Martha leaned back in the comfortable seat. "It would be very helpful if you could grant our technical support team access to any information about the death threats," she said, making a writing gesture in the air to make sure Krisha made a note. He might be acting like they didn't matter, but she wasn't so sure.

She decided it was time to move the conversation on. "What can you tell me about your cat going missing?" Even though she was being totally professional, saying the words sounded surreal to her ears, something Brown seemed to share — if his faintly quizzical look was anything to go by.

Brown sat up straighter and looked at her intently. "I know cats wander off all the time. You hear of them having several different houses where they get fed, but this was different. We've had a Maine Coon since we got married. I don't know if you're familiar with the breed but they're gentle giants. To be honest, George is a bit lazy, it takes a lot to get him out of the house, and as to going walkabout, he's never done that before. He prefers to be with people. My wife isn't feeling too good today so he's in his element, lying on the bed. He adores the kids, and it was they who first alerted us. He always greets them when they come back from school, but there was no sign of him. He was gone for three days, then showed up, right as rain. I only reported it because the kids made such a fuss."

"How did you report him missing? Do you know Assistant Commissioner Jones, by any chance?" Martha fixed him with a direct gaze as she asked the question.

A strange expression floated across Brown's face. Martha was surprised to realise it was sheepishness. "It was only chance I spoke to him at all. A couple of months ago he introduced himself at a seminar organised by Scotland Yard to discuss cybercrime. We were hosting it, which is why I was there.

"Fast forward a few days and just after the cat strolled back in Jones got in touch. We talked about this and that, then, more out of wanting to say something, I mentioned what had happened. I never thought he'd be interested, but he surprised me. Said something about it being a dummy run by people planning something more serious. It felt a bit over the top to me, but he insisted, so I went along with it." He looked between the two women. "It was a bit odd, frankly. I don't know the man, not really, but I got the feeling he was speaking from notes. I really wasn't convinced he believed what he was saying, but he was persistent and gave me the number of Croydon CID, said Sergeant Edwards was best equipped to deal with it."

As she listened in, Martha was wondering about the role of the assistant commissioner. His rank put him in the highest echelon of the top brass, not someone who would normally be expected to get involved in the minutiae of a case. Brown had spoken to him on a couple of occasions, yet there were ordinary police officers who had never spoken to an assistant commissioner during their entire career. She was starting to wonder if her enemies were beginning to flex their muscles again. A sort of 'look how powerful we are' tactic. But why? She put the thought to one side. Mouth suddenly dry, she poured some water and took a small sip.

Brown gave her a moment then carried on. "The PCSO here—" he gestured at Krisha — "turned up and took some notes, and I thought that would be it, until we got the weird text. At which point, I really did think that we needed police involvement. But there was nothing — until today."

Brown paused and Martha saw a flash of fear in his eyes, the concern of a parent for his child. Martha mentally cursed Sergeant Edwards. He wasn't just a poor example of a man, he was a bad copper. He should have escalated the response the moment he heard of the threat.

Martha checked Brown and judged he was OK to carry on. "Could you tell us, in as much detail as possible, about the threat?"

Brown rubbed his hands together making a dry, rasping sound. "It was two days ago that I got a text. At 2.25 p.m. It said: *Next time it's the kids*. I felt like I'd been punched in the stomach. Apparently, I called out because my wife heard and ran in. She read the message and sat straight down. I tried to get hold of the assistant commissioner — he'd given me his mobile — but was astonished to be told he'd retired and could not be contacted. It felt surreal, I'd only spoken to him a short while ago and he'd never mentioned it." Listening to Brown, Martha was privately in agreement about how strange this was, but kept her thoughts to herself. Oblivious to her internal discussion, Brown shook his head in frustration. "I thought about 999 but then wasn't sure. I'd already been told not to do anything that might set alarm bells ringing so I decided to call the Croydon number. This time I explained I'd got the number from an assistant commissioner and was put through to this Sergeant Edwards. He said I was right not to call 999 and promised he would make it a personal priority. He said the response needed to be kept low-key to avoid provoking whoever had sent the text. He said they might disappear — or worse, go on the attack."

The financier looked down at the carpet, then back up at Martha. "I like to think that I'm a decisive man, used to problem solving, but the way he spoke put the wind up me. I don't mind admitting I was scared . . . am scared. That was two days ago and you're the first here." He let out a sigh. "I can't believe I allowed myself to be kept waiting. I'm not boasting when I say that my job gives me a lot of access, but I waited for the police to get back to me. My firm has its own security, so that helped a bit. I suppose I was hoping doing nothing officially would make the threat go away."

Martha nodded sympathetically. "You should never have been put in that situation and it will be taken up, but right now we have a clear priority. The safety of your family. Can you indulge me while we try to extract as much information as we can?" She didn't wait for his approval. "You were quite specific about the time, I take it there's a reason for that."

"That's observant of you," said Brown. "It's just before the New York Stock Exchange opens — in UK time, that is. Most days I can be found in my office, or here, waiting for trading to get underway. It's a habit, really. We employ people to react to what's going on, but if Wall Street's booming, the City will usually be riding the wave."

"We're all creatures of habit," said Martha. "How many people know you do that every day?"

"A lot, is the short answer." Brown shrugged. "We employ dozens and dozens of people, and my office has glass walls so I can be readily seen. And I've been doing it for a long time."

"OK. We're going to need to talk to your people. What about the text itself? Have you kept it and was there anything about it? How many people would have your mobile number?"

"It came from a number I didn't recognise. My people say it was sent from an untraceable burner phone." He looked concerned. "Was it OK for us to make that check?"

Martha held up both hands. "Anyone would have done the same if they could have."

Brown looked relieved. "You asked how many people have my number . . . the answer is a lot. All my people know they can contact me at any time. I encourage it."

Martha glanced at Krisha, who was absorbed with her note-taking, and turned back to Brown. "My chief inspector is taking this very seriously and believes we should be offering you security. Maybe having an officer outside the house. Even better, inside with you guys. My advice is to take it."

The financier didn't hesitate. "No problem with that, so long as you provide a female officer," said Brown. "While I was waiting to hear from you guys, I got my office to find a security outfit, which they did, but they're all men, and my wife would prefer to have a woman on the team."

"I can sympathise with that. I'll see what can be done, but it does depend on who's available with the right training. We have to follow strict protocols," said Martha. "I do have another idea though. There's a woman who lives locally. Full disclosure: she's a good friend of mine, but I can speak from personal experience that she is a top, top operator.

"A few months back she helped me with a very serious problem. She's great with kids and her physical presence is enough to make people cross the road to avoid her. If you like I can call her, and she can come here to meet you."

Brown was enthusiastic about the idea, so Martha called straight away and got through to her friend. She briefly explained the situation. She listened for a moment, then replied. "Thanks Julie. An hour will be great."

Addressing Brown, she said, "She's coming here, and if you guys get on then she can start today. As you probably heard, her name's Julie."

"Can you tell me some more about her?" He was clearly intrigued.

"I don't want to spoil the surprise. But trust me. You'll be in no doubt that she's a bodyguard once you see her."

Martha was about to call it a day when another question came to mind.

"I wanted to go back over your staff. You've said that's all down to your wife, so how does she know who they are?"

Brown looked puzzled, so Martha explained her thinking. "Like today, when Krisha and I arrived, there was a young guy pushing a wheelbarrow. Would your wife know who he was?"

Now Brown was looking more thoughtful. "I think I see where you're going. In the case of the gardening team, that would be the contractor, Steve. He's here today, supervising the new patio."

Martha looked at Krisha. "Now we've raised the question, we'd better double-check and find out who our wheelbarrow guy is, but I'm sure I'm being overcautious."

"No problem," said Krisha. "Do I go back out of the front door to find him?"

Brown shook his head. "Follow me. Steve's working right outside the back door. He's totally bald, you can't miss him."

Martha waited in the study, glad of a moment to gather her thoughts. After a few minutes Krisha was back, her eyes gleaming.

"He said, what young bloke with a wheelbarrow?"

CHAPTER 5

Hedge fund titans are like the best poker players, they know how to hide their thoughts. When you discuss deals worth millions, even billions, it pays to master the art of giving nothing away. And Charles Brown was renowned for his poker face. So, colleagues and competitors alike would have taken great interest in the way he was standing motionless in the doorway to his home with his mouth open. The reason for his unexpected lack of control was Julie, a grinning giant with hair dyed a bright sky blue, who was standing on his doorstep. Instead of asking her in, he stood there thinking Martha had called it just right. Julie loomed over him, and weighing in at 200 pounds of muscle and bone, she was an impressive woman. But Brown also liked her broad smile. If this was who he thought she was, his kids were going to love her.

"You must be Martha's friend?"

Julie inclined her head and offered up her right hand for a fist bump. Brown noted that his fist was dwarfed by her huge paw. "I don't do shakes," said Julie. "People always complain that I'm too rough. This is much better."

Brown got a grip and took a step back from his doorway as he gestured for her to follow him inside. He pulled the door closed and led Julie to his study. "I take it Detective Munro has told you why I'm looking for some help."

Julie's friendly demeanour vanished. "I understand some scumbag is making threats against your kids. I hate people that do that. I'd be glad to help — if you want me."

Now it was Brown's turn to smile. "I think that's almost certainly a given. I gather you have some fairly recent experience in this field."

"You can say that again," said Julie. "I can't give away too much, but safe to say some clown threatened Martha's little girl. Turned out alright in the end, but I saw the pressure it put on Martha. I was part of a protection team that kept her safe. If push comes to shove, I know what I'm there for. I'll always put the children first."

Brown had made his mind up. "If you don't mind, let's get the business part out of the way," said Brown. "When it comes to my family, I don't quibble about the bill. I'm suggesting a three-month contract at a thousand pounds a day, with the first month paid in advance."

"I wasn't expecting anything like that," Julie responded. "Surely that's too much—"

Before she could say more Brown cut her off. "I've got plenty of money . . . I don't have many people like you, and I only have two children."

"When you put it like that . . ." said Julie. "OK, I accept your very generous terms. Now, I understand that you already have security, and you may get police protection."

"My company provided a very good team, ex-military and well trained," explained Brown. "But they're all men, and my wife and kids would prefer a woman. So, you'll concentrate on the family. You'll have to work with the others, but I can't see why that should be an issue."

"I can make that work," said Julie. "We'll have to keep talking. Where are your security people at the moment?"

"They're outside the school, waiting to escort everyone home."

"Walking or driving?"

"Walking, if the weather permits." He gestured at the sun streaming through the window. "I think today will be a walking day."

Julie nodded in agreement, then looked thoughtful. "There is another person I'd like to involve in this. His name is Harry, and although he's been retired for a while, he's as sharp as they come. I'd like him to give things the once over, check for any holes anywhere."

"I've no problem with that. Shall we put him on your terms? I'd be more than happy to do that."

"That won't be necessary," Julie responded. "He's not that motivated by money, says he's got plenty for what he wants."

"Maybe I can make a donation to charity." Brown spread his hands. "I give away a lot of money every year, so would be happy to give to a cause close to his heart."

"You know what, that might appeal to him," said Julie, rubbing her hands together. "Now, when do I get to meet the rest of your family? Maybe I can be here for when they get back from school today? They'll meet me on their turf, which should make it easier."

Ninety minutes later two awed youngsters were getting to know their new minder. "Mummy says if I eat lots of vegetables, I will grow big and strong. Will that make me like you?" said Tom.

Julie, who thought of pepperoni pizza as a vegetable because of the tomato sauce base, looked thoughtful as she picked up the squealing seven-year-old and held him over her head. "I think you might. Then you can do this." She hoisted up his sister with her other hand, leaving their mother, Summer, to look on with a sickly grin.

CHAPTER 6

A day later and Julie was watching with keen interest as an ambulance marked 'private' manoeuvred its way through the school gates and parked up to allow a paramedic to jump down from the passenger side and follow the signs to reception. The school was housed in a palatial Victorian property that had been added to over the decades and now catered for kids from nursery up to eleven years old. Julie had chosen the reception area for her patrol base since it offered the only access to the classrooms, allowing her to keep a close eye on everyone who came and went. Her interest piqued, she moved within listening range of the conversation between the medic and the woman who manned the reception desk.

What she overheard chilled her, making her reach for her phone. She hit Martha's number. The detective answered on the first ring.

"You'd better get down to the reception. Some sicko has sent an ambulance crew claiming they're here to pick up Amelia Brown — who, I might add, is sound as a bell." Julie's calm tone belied how hard her heart was beating.

"I'm coming now. Make sure no one leaves before I get there," said Martha. She was close by because she was running the rule over any weak points which might allow people to get into the school.

Julie tuned back into the conversation between the medic and the receptionist.

"I can assure you no one here called for an ambulance," the receptionist, Mary, was insisting. "We do have an Amelia Brown but she's five years old and twenty minutes ago was running around at break time. She is not an adult and hasn't passed away."

The conversation was becoming surreal, and Julie could sense that Mary was getting in a flap as the reality of what was happening dawned on her.

"It might be best if you rang the head — immediately," interjected Julie, trying to look as reassuring as possible. "I've spoken to the police officer in charge, and she's on her way. She's requested no one leaves. That includes you and the ambulance driver, I'm afraid." Julie aimed a sympathetic smile at the medic, a woman in her mid-thirties, who's name badge identified her as Sarah Gonzales, an employee of the private health company Clinical Care. The woman took a deep breath and a defiant expression appeared on her face. She opened her mouth to speak but a fierce glare from Julie made her change her mind.

"I recognise this is a pain. But the cops are on the way. Just to help you understand, it may be that your being sent here is linked to threats made against a couple of the children."

Gonzales visibly deflated as Julie's information sank in, and she stayed put without any comment.

Minutes later, they both swung round to look at the entrance as Martha raced in with Krisha close behind. The detective scanned the area as she marched up to Julie, who pointed at Gonzales.

Fixing her gaze on the paramedic she said, "What can you tell me about how you came to be sent here? Please take your time, I'd like you to talk me through every step of the process."

Gonzales spread her hands. "There's not a great deal to tell you. The process is designed to be quick and simple. We get a warning beep in the cab which lets us know we're about to receive a text alert, asking us to ring into ambulance control. That's obviously a job for the passenger — me in this case — since our emergency response vehicles always have a crew of two. This time was same as always. I called in and was told that due to pressure on NHS services we needed to help. It's not that uncommon, in all honesty. We were told to come here to pick up the body of an adult female, Mrs Amelia Brown, who had passed away this morning." She glanced between Martha and Julie. "That's all I can tell you."

Martha looked frustrated — she'd been hoping for some sort of clue. "So, nothing out of the ordinary? Not even some tiny thing?"

"All normal. Like every day," said Gonzales.

"And you didn't think it was odd?"

Sarah pouted. "Not really. In this job you learn that death can happen anywhere, and for any reason. I imagine there are plenty of adults who work here."

"And nothing surprising about not having an exact cause of death?"

"No, not at all," replied Gonzales. "In these circumstances our job is to collect the body and take them to a hospital, where the cause of death can be established by a doctor."

"Who assigns you to each job?"

"That would be our central control, which sounds very grand but is really only a room in the basement of one of our hospitals near Chelsea Bridge," said Gonzales. Then she paused and made a quiet 'ooh' sound.

"What is it?" asked Martha, her pulse racing.

"It may be nothing, but I just remembered that I didn't recognise the voice of the woman I spoke to. While you get a lot of different staff around at weekends, during the week it tends to be the same people. I quite often speak to a Scottish man, Peter."

"Was there anything distinctive about this new voice?"

"I'm sorry." Gonzales shook her head.

"Do you record messages or conversations when they come in?"

"Yes, we do," said Gonzales, looking stressed that she had forgotten this detail.

"Brilliant. Can you play it back from the ambulance recorder?" The paramedic nodded before leading the way. Martha stopped to glance at Julie. "While I listen in, can you go and check on Amelia and Tom? Once I get clear of this, we can call their dad."

Julie cracked her knuckles. "On my way."

As Julie disappeared, Martha called Krisha over to a quiet spot. "We need to make sure we check out this ambulance crew. Can you get on to Tony to do an urgent background check?"

"Are you treating them as suspects?"

"Suspects is going too far, but we can't dismiss them either."

"OK, and we should find someone in the ambulance service who can confirm this story about helping out the NHS. You know, this thing about sharing ambulance services with the private sector."

"Yes, we should," said Martha. "I should have thought of that myself." She stole a glance at Krisha; the woman was growing on her.

CHAPTER 7

Martha listened to the recording three times but had to concede there was little she could extract from it. If there were some clues hidden in the background, it was going to need some specialist audio skills to pull them out.

The speaker had a strong London accent, and Martha formed an impression of a younger woman, maybe in her early twenties, although she was wary of placing too much on that: voices could be deceptive.

Giving up on the recording she went and asked the driver and Gonzales to wait until their IDs had been confirmed, then she walked back into the reception, where she found the unsurprisingly agitated head teacher, Tracey Hardiman.

"What is going on here? I'm being told there is an ambulance for one of my pupils," said Tracey, who'd started talking the moment Martha appeared.

"That's what we're trying to get to the bottom of," answered Martha. "It appears to be some sort of trick."

Tracey looked like she was about to respond angrily when she made a clear effort to calm down.

"I get very defensive about my children. Is there anything I can do to help?"

Martha was saved from responding when Julie stepped back into the now crowded reception area. Her sheer bulk seemed to calm the head further. "The kids are both fine," Julie announced.

"Good. Now, let me phone Mr Brown," said Martha.

Brown picked up on the first ring and Martha quickly filled him in. He gasped when she told him about the ambulance arriving.

"That's terrible! My wife and I are on the way now."

"Maybe count to ten first," said Martha. "We've got everything covered here, as worrying as it is. With that in mind, if you turn up unexpectedly might it worry your children?"

"Let me check with my wife," said Brown.

She could hear him talking quietly to a slightly more urgent female voice, then he was back on the line. "Can you confirm the kids are unaware of this right now?"

"I can," said Martha.

There was another muffled conversation. Martha could make out enough to tell that Summer was not thrilled at being told what to do. "OK, we'll stay here. But could you put Julie on? I think it will help to reassure her."

Moments later Julie was talking to Summer. "They have no idea what is going on. I've been to see them myself and they couldn't be happier. Look, no one would dream of telling a mum what to do with her own children, but this really is one to occupy the grown-ups, not the kids. I promise that if anything changes, I will personally call you straight away."

Summer reluctantly accepted. "OK. I agree there's no point unsettling them. But if anything happens . . . I'm coming."

Julie passed the phone back to Martha as Charles came back on. "I'm glad you introduced us to Julie, without her being on site there's no chance Summer would have stayed away. She's only taking your advice because she trusts both of you. Don't let us down." He was making his position clear.

The connection went silent, giving Martha a moment to reflect that she would have said the same thing. His voice grabbed her attention back. "Would you mind coming to my house at some point, just to fill us in in person. If that's OK? It would reassure both of us."

"No problem," said Martha. She wanted to speak face to face anyway as she kept thinking about his lack of concern over making enemies. He'd been too quick to dismiss it. She needed to press him again, make sure he wasn't holding anything back, either intentionally or unintentionally. He might be right that most of the world reflexively hated 'hedgies', but that didn't mean the whole issue should be dismissed.

She also wanted to nudge him to think carefully about his staff. Could one of them have come up with this wicked scheme? Targeting his children felt up close and personal — someone wanted him to really suffer. Or maybe it was aimed at his wife. She knew from personal experience how devastating it was for any mother to imagine her children coming to harm.

That concern led her to worry that with all the investigative time already lost, the person or persons making the threat might be about to escalate their campaign. She felt a fresh wave of anger towards Sergeant Edwards. The man was a dangerous menace. Before she could get any gloomier, Julie chose that moment to step closer, reminding Martha that anyone wishing harm to the children would need to get through her formidable friend first. But not even Julie was bulletproof. Did the family need armed protection? She'd bring it up with Tony when she rang to update him on the ambulance stunt.

She glanced at Tracey, who was looking very unhappy, which didn't surprise her. If this was her reaction now, having armed police on site might tip her over the edge. Would she insist that the children were taken out of school in case they caused problems for the other pupils? From her own recent experience, she knew how important it had been for Betty's routine to be kept as normal as possible. If push came to shove then the head teacher would get her own way and Martha would understand. She hoped it wouldn't come to that. She really needed to talk to the chief inspector.

* * *

"Pulling a stunt like that is awful," said Tony, after Martha had filled him in. "When I saw you were the caller, I knew something must have happened, but I didn't imagine it could be this. Do the parents know? They must be reeling."

"They are . . . they were going to rush straight down but I very gently suggested we had it under control and them unexpectedly appearing might alert the kids that something is going on. I advised them to stick to their normal routine, but maybe I should reconsider. What's your take?"

"It's never easy to judge these things, but you were in the right place to make the call," said Tony, who was looking out of his office window at an uninspiring view of South London traffic. "I can imagine that mum and dad are in shock, which means they might change their minds at any moment, so keep that in mind."

Martha carefully glanced around before replying. What she was about to say could not be overheard. To be on the safe side, she walked outside. "Do you think we need to consider stepping it up by including a firearms team to protect the family? My friend Julie, the one I told you about, is here and guarding the children, but it feels like the threat is escalating."

She could hear a sharp intake of breath as Tony took on her comment. "Good question, Martha. I'll pass it up the line to the area commander. There's no doubt this ambulance development takes the threat level upwards, but my instinct says the existing presence is enough . . . for now. But let's get a second opinion."

Martha was happy with his response and moved the conversation on to her fears that Mr Brown wasn't thinking clearly when it came to spotting who might be behind this.

"That's an interesting observation. I suspect you're right about him. I spent a couple of years with the Fraud Squad and talked to a few very successful bankers. They were brilliant at what they did, no doubt about it, but it seemed some of them had become immune to how much anger was directed their way. Or that's how it seemed to me. Keep pushing him, that's all you can do.

"Now, on a practical level you're going to need help doing a deep dive into the family background. I'm going to assign you more people."

"Thank you, sir," said Martha. "Does this remain my case, then?" She had wondered if control would pass to a more senior colleague.

"You stay in charge, at least for now," said Tony. "That's the best I can offer you. At the moment, with the threats escalating, it will attract attention. But don't worry, if a more senior officer is put in charge, you're staying on the case. Let's face it, if you hadn't taken this seriously, we wouldn't have known what was going on. I'll have an incident room set up here at Walworth Road. Make sure you keep me in the loop. In the meantime, keep Krish, and I'll get a patrol car to do a couple of drive-pasts. The least we can do is put on a bit of a show."

Martha had one other urgent matter. "You know the Brown family has brought in private security. Apart from my friend?"

"I do. He's using some very exclusive firm that provides bodyguards to City hotshots," said the chief inspector. "Those guys are all ex-military, well trained and licensed. Are you asking because you're worried about something?"

"In a way, yes, although worried is too strong a word," said Martha. "I need to know what their rules of engagement are. I don't want some private outfit getting in the middle of a police operation."

"Yes, I see what you're getting at. Talk to Mr Brown. If you think it would help, call me and I'll explain his troops need to remember they must act within the law and should treat you as the senior officer."

"Thank you, sir. One last thing. I haven't the slightest doubt Julie's left that part of her life behind, but can I double-check you're OK having an ex-con on board?"

"I appreciate your concern, that speaks volumes. But you've shown me that your instincts are right on the money, and let's face it, everyone deserves a chance of redemption."

Martha had been holding her breath. "That means a lot. When we have more time, I'll tell you all about how I entrusted Julie with my own daughter's life."

CHAPTER 8

Martha didn't get a chance to knock on the front door before it was flung open to reveal a furious-looking Brown.

"Somebody's attacked my car," he said, walking down the steps, gesturing for them to turn round. He led the way to a black SUV, which Martha saw had a Bentley badge.

"Look at this," Brown said, gesturing at the front tyres where someone had slashed at the thick rubber. "Both tyres ruined. I don't care about the damage. I can get that fixed. What I'd like to know is, what is going on? One of my security team spotted it when they inspected the car just now, before I took it out." He threw his hands in the air. "They've been here for a while. Not sure why it took them so long to check my vehicle."

Martha agreed: this lack of attention wasn't reassuring.

She glanced to her left and was pleased to see that Krisha was taking pictures. "Our wheelbarrow man has to be top of the list for suspects," she said, walking over.

"Exactly what I was thinking. Any news on that front?"

"Nothing yet," said Martha. "The ID we worked on is queued up to go through facial recognition, although it's quite a long queue."

"Well, I'm sure it's a good likeness," said Krisha.

Martha patted her arm and walked back to Brown, who had an apologetic look on his face.

"Sorry to get shouty," said the hedge fund boss. "First the ambulance and now this." His expression became sombre. "You can replace a tyre, not so easy with people."

Martha thought he looked smaller somehow — not surprising the way incidents were piling up. "If you don't mind, could I ask a few questions about this—" she gestured at the car — "then can we go back in the house?"

She didn't wait for a reply, quickly establishing that Brown hadn't even looked at the car until twenty minutes ago. Before that the last time he'd been near the vehicle was the previous afternoon, which left a biggish window for the slasher to strike. Martha was thinking they'd probably acted under the cover of darkness. It's what she would have done. For some reason thoughts of Harry, the retired South London gangster who had become her friend and mentor, intruded on her mind. She suppressed a smile as she imagined him arching an eyebrow and professing, "*It always helps to wait for dark when you're up to no good.*" He was the man she was going to bring in to find out more about this mysterious assistant commissioner. Harry could be trusted to get on with his task and only report in when he had something solid. She wondered if this 'shadow investigation' was going to be the key to everything.

Realising she'd allowed herself to drift, she squared her shoulders. "Do you use this car to drive the kids to school?"

"Not often," said Brown. "They usually walk, but if it's raining or something and they need to be driven, my wife takes them in the estate." He gestured at a gleaming blue-grey Volvo parked further along the road. "The Volvo is more suitable."

Martha thought — but didn't say — that he probably wanted to keep his flashy vehicle a kid-free zone. instead, she asked, "Do you have a driver?"

"Not often, only for evening events, otherwise we both like to drive," said Brown.

There was something about the answer that nagged at Martha, but whatever it was remained stubbornly beyond reach. She filed it away for later consideration and asked more questions, establishing that nothing like the slashing had happened before, at least not since the Browns had moved in.

"This is *Dulwich*," he responded.

Martha's thoughts turned to Harry once more, but she kept that to herself.

"What about that mysterious man with his wheelbarrow? You must be thinking he had something to do with it? He might have been using that wheelbarrow to carry whatever he used on my tyres."

"We certainly can't rule anything out at this stage. We're doing everything we can to establish his identity."

Not wanting to get drawn into a prolonged discussion about suspects, Martha walked back towards Krisha and suggested she go door to door on the off chance someone had seen something. It would also give them an opportunity to start hoovering up all the CCTV in the area, something she'd been wanting to get stuck into from the beginning. At least now she would have the resources to go through everything collected in the field, an absolute luxury for any investigator.

Martha and Brown made their way back into the house, the detective determined to press him about the death threats. As he led her back to the office, she could sense the nervous energy that was pouring off him.

"Perhaps if I get straight to the point," said Martha. "I need you to think again about your answer to a question I put to you earlier."

"You want me to think about any enemies I might have," said Brown. "I could tell you didn't think much of my previous answer. I have been thinking about it, but it comes back to the same answer . . . show me a hedge funder who doesn't have enemies. But I find it hard to believe my 'haters' are especially violent."

"I totally accept that," said Martha. "And you mentioned you suffered on social media. But just because

40

something happens all the time, that doesn't mean you should dismiss it. Look, there's no polite way of saying this: is it possible that you've become desensitised to the threats?" She saw him stiffen and quickly hurried on. "I'm not suggesting you've got careless, far from it. But the person behind this knows your routine, which might suggest it's someone who knows you, or at least has access to your day-to-day schedule."

"You mean like a member of the domestic staff?" said Brown.

"Could be, yes," replied Martha. "Not part of your inner circle, but someone who can get close to you without drawing attention."

"That's a good point," said Brown as he began pacing round the room.

"I think you need to give me two lists," said Martha. "One with your domestic people on it, and one with work staff. Plus contact details. Most importantly, how many of them would have access to this office."

"I'll do that right away," said Brown, sitting down and reaching for his laptop. "I would stress though that anyone who works for me is vetted, and that is *anyone*."

Martha mulled this over. "Background checks are important, but there are always ways round them."

While she was talking, he'd been tapping away, and in no time at all the information was coming off the printer.

"Does that include contact details?" asked Martha, looking at the printer, which was a vastly superior model to that she was used to.

Brown tapped his forehead. "I never forget a detail." He handed the lists over, and a quick glance told Martha that, assuming all this information was correct, Brown had formidable recall. She was going to need all the help that Tony could provide in order to get through them.

She was getting to her feet when that nagging thought about the car morphed into a serious question.

"Has your wife been out in her car since yesterday?"

"No. Not even the school run. In fact, it was your lady, Julie, who walked the kids to school today."

His answer made Martha go cold. She reached for her phone, she needed to get hold of Krisha. "Are you anywhere near Mrs Brown's car — the Volvo?" Martha asked after her colleague picked up. Relieved that Krisha wasn't close, she said, "Stay well back and do what you can to keep people away. I'm calling in the bomb squad."

CHAPTER 9

Martha watched intently as the explosives officers went through their routines. First a detailed inspection had been carried out by a robot "sniffer" dog, which had identified a suspicious package under the car. Next a bomb disposal expert, clad in heavy duty armour, went in. The female officer slid sideways until she was level with the device. Martha shut her eyes and thought there was nothing which could have persuaded her to do that. Even standing well back and in no personal danger she was bathed in cold sweat.

The closest houses had been evacuated and behind her were some of the residents, expressing every emotion from fear to fury. The expert was taking her time, lying on her back as she examined something under the driver's side. The tension was unbearable, and several times Martha found herself standing on the tips of her toes as her raised adrenaline levels made her fidget nervously. Nearby was a group that included a shaken-looking couple, and slightly apart from them, the domestic staff, looking grim and frightened. Martha wondered how many of them would be turning up for work again after this. She wouldn't blame them if they scattered. Dealing with bombs was not in the average job description, especially not on minimum wage. Fortunately, it was a warm day, as everyone had been rushed out of the closest houses with no chance of grabbing a coat.

Martha turned her attention back to the Browns and could see the situation was taking a huge toll — little wonder, given the way the pressure was mounting by the day. She noted that Summer Brown had red-rimmed eyes as though tears were never far away, while her husband was grim-faced and held himself stiffly, although he made a visible attempt to rally as Martha stepped over.

"How did you work it out about the bomb?" Brown said. "You seemed to pluck it out of thin air."

"It was a guess, really," said Martha, not wanting to claim any credit. "Something was nagging at me — it felt carefully coordinated, like you were being pushed in one direction. Someone really wanted you to take the Volvo. I couldn't be sure, but once I had the thought there was no way I was taking any risks."

Mr Brown reached out and patted Martha's shoulder in mute thanks. His wife started to sob quietly as the implications sank in. "Someone was hoping to force us into that car this morning," she said. Her voice was little more than a whisper.

Martha wished she could console them, but sometimes there were no words. The best she could do was leave them in peace and get on with catching whoever was behind this.

Martha checked her watch for the third time — another five minutes had gone past. It felt like longer. Finally, the bomb expert dragged herself, and an oblong-shaped container about the size of a large box of chocolates, clear of the car. Overcoming her primal fear, Martha walked towards the expert, Major Rachel Daly. Despite the major assuring her that everything was under control, her lizard brain was letting the side down. It was strongly suggesting that she 'run away now and talk later'. She swallowed hard, and hoped no one picked up on her sudden indecision. She was helped when the major offered a fist bump.

"You never forget your first," she said with a wicked grin that put things in perspective.

Martha couldn't help looking bashful. "I was that obvious?"

"Only to someone who knew what they were looking for, and I would have been more worried if you'd been excited. Defusing bombs shouldn't be on anyone's bucket list."

"Well, I don't know how you guys do it," Martha admitted. "I don't mind telling you, but I was wetting myself back there. You're incredibly brave."

The woman ran her hand through her sweat-dampened hair. "Someone has to do it." Despite her self-deprecatory tone, Martha sensed the inner steel which allowed her to operate in such a dangerous field.

If she'd known the major better, Martha might have offered her a hug, but instead she asked, "I take it that you have everything under control?"

"Yup," said the major, as she stood holding the 'device': a wooden box, about the size of a typical hardback novel, with a hinged lid. She held it up for inspection, opening the box to display a pile of black powder with a familiar smell.

"Am I right in thinking that smells like fireworks?" said Martha.

"The lady wins a prize," came the reply.

"What sort of damage would that amount have done? It looks about the size of a small bag of flour," said Martha.

"Not much, really," was Daly's reply. "A lot of smoke and maybe a small bang, but that would be it." She shrugged. "I suppose it would have been a major distraction and it might have made the driver lose control, but only briefly. Most likely they would have slammed on the brakes."

"So, what was the point?" asked Martha, who then answered her own question as she glanced around. "It must have been to grab our attention, make sure we don't ignore them, whoever 'them' is."

Before she could explore this idea further, she spotted Krisha waving at her urgently. She walked over. The PCSO was grinning enthusiastically and Martha thought, yet again, she was lucky to have her.

"We may have some CCTV footage." For the second time in a few minutes Martha felt an urge to hug someone. She restricted herself to a broad smile.

"Does it feature a guest appearance by wheelbarrow man?"

CHAPTER 10

Maria Nightingale found the routine of everyday life tedious at the best of times. Recently, it was weighing on her more than ever. Her husband was annoying, and her children were at the age when they were only interested in social media. She even found her friends painful, most of them obsessed with trying to defy the ageing process and complaining if they put on so much as an ounce in weight. "It's alright for you, darling," one acquaintance had whined. "You're already thin and rich."

Try eating less, fatso, she thought. But it was health concerns that had spelled the death knell for the one thing she still looked forward to: long lunches featuring espresso martinis. Maria could testify it had an anaesthetising effect which dulled the boredom of listening to another mother boasting about her children, and it looked better than guzzling neat vodka.

Desperate for something to do, Maria had considered going back to work, but that filled her with dread. Marriage seemed to offer a way out and she decided to give child-rearing a try, but she quickly found that tedious; not even a lovely Victorian mansion in Dulwich could keep her engaged. Starting to feel desperate, she turned to exercise

— lots of exercise. This was when her real problems began. She'd gone for a short run when she had the accident. A silly thing really. She was jogging into Dulwich Park when she misjudged the kerb as she moved from the road to the grass. She overstretched her right leg, planting it in the softer ground and then falling over to her left with her knee taking all her weight. It lasted for a heartbeat — long enough to change her life.

She had properly smashed her knee. At the hospital they had talked of a ruptured cruciate and wrecked cartilage. But none of that mattered, as the doctors had introduced her to the delights of opioid pain relief. After the first injection all her troubles had floated away, leaving her feeling more relaxed than she could recall. It was addiction at first injection. By the time she got out of hospital, there was only one thing on her mind: *give me more drugs*.

With a successful banker for a husband, money was no object, and she quickly found a couple of sympathetic private doctors who helped out with prescriptions. Fentanyl patches gave her the base and she could top up with codeine, washed down with vodka, as needed. She was careful. She knew she was an addict, but was determined no one would find out.

* * *

In her younger days Audrey Taylor had carved out a niche as a cleaner catering to wealthy young bankers who lived in the heart of the City. She always turned up, never even taking a holiday break, and never tried to engage with her clients on a social level, something they all valued.

Except one. Mr Proudfoot. Two years ago, when she was still well enough to work, she'd responded to an advert and been surprised when he had conducted the interview himself. His current home was an apartment in Bankside. It was a few steps from the Millennium Bridge and Shakespeare's Globe, and she never tired of the startling view across the Thames to the dome of St Paul's Cathedral. It was a good place to share secrets. Had she been a little more self-aware she would have noticed the traffic was one-way.

Then ill-health struck with a frightening rapidity that saw her quickly lose her ability to work. When she had told Proudfoot, he was generous. He insisted she take three months' pay and gave her a contact number to call 'when you have problems'.

When Imelda came up with her publishing idea, Mummy knew exactly who to call. Proudfoot had promised to think about it, admitting that he knew lots of people in the financial industry, who in turn knew publishers. It was a matter of finding the right door to lean on. The dinner party circuit in Dulwich would be a good place to start. As promised, he delivered some names and said he was working on a plan to get their help and was passing the names on so that Audrey could get Imelda to do some digging. "Get her to check out where they live. How many kids? Pets? That sort of thing. You never know when it might be helpful." Although Proudfoot warned her there could be no guarantees, she convinced herself the plan would work. When her dreams of being the mother of a successful literary figure crashed to the ground she flew into an intense rage.

She'd called Proudfoot and ranted and raved. He listened quietly, and when she finally stopped speaking, he responded.

"I had hoped it wouldn't come to this but now it has I can tell you a secret. The same people who have let you down have also let me down on a rather large financial arrangement." He stoked her resentment with a reminder that one of the Dulwich A-list, Charles Brown, was wealthy enough and influential enough to open any door for Imelda with a quiet word in the right ear.

Also namechecked was the 'junkie' Maria Nightingale. "That woman should have told her husband about Imelda; he would have got her a job with one text message."

Her head spinning and her heart pounding with excitement, Audrey agreed to wait. Proudfoot assured her that "events are already in motion. They will pay for letting us both down."

CHAPTER 11

Proudfoot called back within the week. He was ready to go. Audrey's concern over her daughter's reaction evaporated after Imelda broke into a round of applause once her mother told her about the conversation.

"Mummy, that's quite brilliant. Let me get you another glass of sherry. I think I might have a glass of wine myself, there's a lot to take on board and you want me to start with the cats in a couple of weeks, so I need to get a wiggle on." It was an expression Audrey hated but she let it pass this time.

Imelda was blissfully unaware of this potential for friction, since she was so focused on the work ahead. By the next morning she had carried out a recce, guided by her mother, and felt she understood the lay of the land. Now for the cats, a job which would prove simple enough even if she couldn't quite fathom why she was doing it — instead she focused on the expectation that it would cause confusion and misery, which she regarded as good enough reasons in their own right. As an added bonus she could prod her mother, who despite claiming it was her own plan, was a little shaky on the details.

"Tell me again, Mummy. You want me to take the cats away and then bring them back? It seems a lot of fuss over nothing."

Audrey wasn't sure either, but she was stuck with it now. "Smoke and mirrors, my darling," she finally improvised. "You can never have enough smoke and mirrors."

Imelda shrugged. It still made no sense, but she actually didn't care. Once the cats were out of the way she could move on to the fun bit: frightening people. She was discovering a whole new side to herself. Even better, the prospect of murder had been raised. Not straight away, but soon. This really raised the stakes, and she rolled the word around inside her head. It had a finality to it which was entirely in keeping. She was also enjoying a most unusual feeling. She was important . . . no, make that *essential*. There was no way her mother was physically up to any of the tasks, especially murder. And definitely not in her current state. That was for a stronger, younger woman like Imelda. She liked the idea and even came up with a name for herself, Imelda the Wicked, or maybe, Wicked Imelda, maybe just Wicked. She didn't need to decide yet, she could have a think about it.

A few weeks later Imelda had taken all the cats and then brought them back. Now she could look forward to a campaign in which Wicked would inflict fear and death.

Emboldened by her newfound confidence, Imelda had seized control of the timings for the plan. Days earlier Audrey had produced the door keys and information that would get her into the first house. More importantly, it would bring her to the first victim. Any questions about where her mother had got everything from were shoved to one side, at least for now. She had already scouted the precise location of the security cameras. It was all very well Audrey saying no one paid attention to the domestic staff, she wasn't the one going inside the house. Imelda had spotted that a couple of the cameras would be bypassed simply by using the side door, while one more would need a small nudge to be redirected to a view of a flower bed and nothing more.

Although she was making all the moves, she made the effort to keep Audrey informed, but her mother was spending a lot of time asleep. She hadn't even eaten her breakfast this morning. Even with her mother's silence, the clock ticked on, and at last it was time for action. As she left Imelda was pleased to hear her mother calling out "good luck".

The first target, Maria Nightingale, was also doing her bit — albeit unknowingly. Her knee was proving especially troublesome, and she had gone for the 'pain relief' a little earlier than usual. By 1.30 p.m. she was in her bedroom and ready to wash down the codeine with a very stiff vodka. The combo kicked in faster than normal, thanks to Imelda — currently hiding out in one of the spare bedrooms — who had laced the alcohol with a hefty dose of liquid morphine.

Twenty minutes after hearing Maria shut her door, Imelda judged the time was right and carefully let herself into the bedroom to find Maria sprawled across the bed, with a senseless smile on her face. For a moment Imelda panicked. She worried that Maria might pass out before she could finish the plan.

She needed to hurry, and leaned forward to whisper in Maria's ear.

"Mrs Nightingale, you must come and look. From your window you can see that all the flowers are in bloom." Among the information she'd been handed was the fact that Nightingale was obsessed with flowers and instructed the gardener to plant them in every available space in her garden.

At first there was no response and she worried again that she had overdone the drugs. If she had, she'd miss the chance of getting up close and personal. She was suddenly filled with rage. This bloody woman was threatening to spoil her fun because she was too out of it. She went to slap her face but just pulled back. "No marks," she reminded herself.

"Get up, wake up, you bloody bitch," she hissed. "Come on you bitch. It's time to die."

The threats seemed to get through. Maria started to mutter. It was faint but she was saying "flowers". Cautiously, Imelda tried to pull her into a sitting position. It was slow work but bit by bit, Maria sat up straight, eventually able to support herself. The morphine was doing its job, leaving her enough awareness to respond to spoken instructions.

Imelda stepped back and looked at her closely. The next bit would be so much easier if Maria could get to her feet. "Can you manage to walk to the window? I know your knee hurts, but the flowers really are so beautiful from up here."

Agonisingly slowly she got to her feet, swaying in an invisible breeze. Imelda had got the dose about right, she thought triumphantly — just at the point where Maria would do as she asked without noticing she was a stranger. "A few more steps and then you can rest your hands on the windowsill."

The bedroom was huge, and she needed to guide her across the deep-pile carpet. At one point Maria lurched forward alarmingly, but with the kind of wobbly balance only a drunk can muster, she pulled herself upright and tottered across the room.

With her hands resting on the windowsill, Maria leaned out to look at the flowers. Standing close behind, Imelda unconsciously flexed her fingers as she judged that a firm push on Maria's bottom would do the trick.

"Goodbye, Maria," she whispered as her victim dropped fifteen feet, landing headfirst. Death was quick as her spinal cord was instantly severed. She never made a sound, and had they known, her family would have been slightly soothed to learn that in her final moments, Maria thought she was flying.

Imelda made her way downstairs. She wondered how long it would be before the body was discovered. Stepping outside she pulled up the hood on her jacket and casually walked away. Not a trace of remorse entered her thoughts. Instead she was thinking, *You sure had a bony arse, lady.*

CHAPTER 12

As the hoax bomb was carried away, Martha was forced to consider the one issue she had been doing her best to ignore. Namely, there was a level of weirdness about this which made her wonder how much of it was aimed at her. In other words, using the Brown family as a means to an end, to get at Martha. She knew she was being paranoid — astonishingly self-centred, some might say — but as Julie said, even paranoids have enemies, and thanks to her now deceased father's work as the scourge of corruption, Martha had seemed to inherit all of his. Not that long ago she'd have considered such an idea as verging on the deranged. But her own experience proved that bad things could, and did, happen.

She kept coming back to one issue — how had an assistant commissioner become so closely involved from the start when this was the most mundane of incidents and should not have called for police scrutiny? She had to consider whether Heath Jones had known in advance that this was going to escalate from the frankly ludicrous to death threats and explosive devices.

The big question was, why? And it was that which was troubling her. Because if she added in the actions of Sergeant Edwards it was starting to look like someone was pulling strings to put Martha at the heart of events. And if it was her father's tainted legacy that was once again in play — he'd allowed too many ruthless criminals to go free in a headlong assault on the highest echelons — that could only be bad news for her, her family and her friends.

Before this case she had been starting to think she could put all of her father's secrets behind her, safe in the knowledge they were dead and buried. Now she had the strongest sense that a very deadly enemy was still out there and still operating in the belief that Martha had something that he, or she, desperately wanted. This hidden enemy suspected she had information which proved they had been in the pay of the police. A dangerous thing to be said about a career criminal. The bitter irony was that Martha didn't possess such information but found herself in the impossible position of trying to prove a negative.

She had already been set up and sent to a high-security prison, where it was intended she should suffer a savage beating — one that would most likely leave her dead. She was only saved thanks to the intervention of her great friend Harry. Using his extensive criminal contacts picked up during a career as a gangland enforcer, Harry had managed to reach out to Julie, already serving time, and she had agreed to keep Martha safe. Which was just as well since within hours of Martha arriving at HMP *Bronzefield*, Julie had already stepped in to thwart the first of several attacks. Fortunately, within days, Martha's legal team had secured her release from prison. That had been a year ago, and during this time Martha had started to hope that the worst was over, but now she had to face the ugly truth. One or more of her father's enemies had her in their sights. Her head might say there was no evidence, but her heart knew otherwise. She might not know all those involved, but she needed to consider one name — Neil Thompson. Current events suggested he was the one operating behind the scenes. She knew precious little about him other than he was an enemy to take very seriously.

She steeled herself. The sensible plan was for her to run two campaigns. The first would be the official police inquiry she was currently in charge of. The second would be much more secretive, and she was going to need Harry's help once more — along with the rest of her team, Julie and maybe her ex-husband Justin, the father of their daughter Betty. She wished she had all three of them right now, but she was going to have to wait. Justin was working on a project that was important to his future and would benefit Betty too. She was desperate to give him time, although she knew that might not be possible much longer.

She was going to need to be at the top of her game. With the police investigation she now had two serious threats against the Brown family: the text and the bomb threat. Both needed to be given equal weight. Yes, she had a lot on her plate, but at least the hard-driving Krisha was making sure Martha focused on the immediate issues. Anyone who claimed PCSOs were glorified traffic wardens should meet her new colleague.

Martha snapped out of introspection as she became aware Krisha was trying to attract her attention. Her heart rate went up as she went to find out what Krisha was so excited about.

"I thought you'd want to see this immediately." It turned out that while the area was being evacuated Krisha had persuaded one of the homeowners to bring footage from their security camera with them. Martha was introduced to a Harvey and Margaret Hazel. He was a big man with a fierce expression, the reason for which was about to come clear. He lived next door to the Browns and had returned from holiday with his wife a week ago, a timeframe that was also about to become more significant.

"After I checked my CCTV footage, I called 101 and was told an officer would come round to look at it," said Harvey Hazel. "That was six days ago, and I've heard nothing since."

Martha smiled apologetically. This was becoming an annoyingly repetitive soundtrack to the investigation.

"Thank you for having the patience to stay with us," said Martha. It was all she could say.

Luckily, Harvey seemed in a conciliatory mood. He waved a hand at her, signalling the battle was over.

"Well, let's look at what you've got," said Martha.

"It's not brilliant footage," said Krisha. "Mr Hazel has a camera above his front door. It just reaches round to the boundary of the Brown house."

Taking this as his cue, Mr Hazel handed Martha a laptop. "Hit play."

Martha watched as a dark-clothed figure stood with its back to the camera, looking into the Brown family home. As she watched, the figure lifted a box from the ground and upended it to release a cat. Then the figure moved out of vision.

"It looks like we have our cat-snatcher," said Martha. "Any observations?"

"I'm not sure if it's a man or a woman," said Krisha.

"I can't tell either," said Martha. She pulled Krisha out of earshot of the homeowner. "We need to get that to technical support, see if they can do anything to enhance the quality. It might be our wheelbarrow man. Tell them we have a possible terrorist element to this."

"It's a good job you took this seriously from the beginning," said Krisha. "The Met might have ended up looking pretty stupid if not for you. I'd love to see the expression on Sergeant Edwards' face when he finds out he assigned you to lead a major investigation."

As they were talking the familiar wail of an ambulance siren could be heard in the background. It was out of sight but close by, in the heart of the village. For some reason the sound made Martha shiver.

"Someone just walked over my grave," she said in response to a raised eyebrow from her colleague.

"That's the sort of thing my mum says," said Krisha, which Martha wasn't entirely sure how to take, but before she could consider it, Krisha's phone beeped. She checked her messages and nodded with approval.

"Operations has declared the area safe again. I'm going to keep trying for any footage. I might need to come back this evening, in case people are out. Is that OK with you?"

"No problem with you working but I can't promise overtime, if you're OK with that?"

Krisha didn't hesitate. "It'll be good experience. I want to be an actual police officer one day."

The more she saw of the hard-working woman the more impressed Martha was, which made her think of their boss. "I'd better talk to Tony again, let him know the latest and find out if there is any official overtime."

* * *

The chief inspector listened quietly as she briefed him on developments over the phone. "You've done well, you and Krisha both. I'm pleased to say you remain in charge, at least for now. The fact that a device was found at Brown's home does raise the stakes, but fortune is favouring you as there's no one immediately available at the rank of inspector or above. It comes down to my judgement call, and I am happy that you are up to the job . . . which means that for now, you're the boss. Let's make sure we all keep talking and we should get through."

"Thank you, sir," said Martha. She'd prepped herself to fear the worst, so to get a positive result was fantastic. She hoped the excitement wasn't too obvious in her voice.

"Use me as a sounding board if you have any doubts, but so far your handling of the case has been exemplary," said Tony. "I'm guessing you learned a few lessons from the last major investigation you were involved in."

She knew he was making an oblique reference to the unofficial investigation which had seen her jailed and almost cost Martha her life. His next comment gave her pause for thought.

"Your 'friend', Sergeant Edwards," added Tony. "He seems to have suddenly retired. No warning. No drinks party. Just left the building. It feels a bit odd to me, but I can't really ask around because an officer of my rank asking questions will get noticed, and I think we should keep it on the down-low for now. If you know someone you can talk to, it might be useful to know what's going on. Obviously don't let it get in the way."

Martha was glad that Green couldn't see her response. His comments had made her go quite pale and she was blinking rapidly. She had to swallow several times before she trusted herself to reply.

"That is interesting. He had a nice little number there. Regular hours, not too much work. I can't see a man like that walking away before he's ready."

It was probably just as well she kept her thoughts unspoken. She had a bad feeling about this development. Only someone very senior could have forced him out. It was too much of a coincidence that a few days ago the sergeant was giving her the runaround. Now his scheme to give her a hard time had failed, he was out.

It was exactly that type of hidden power which had touched her life so recently. She'd come close to being killed. As much as she had prayed Neil Thompson was out of their lives, there was a sense of déjà vu about the way events were moving, and she couldn't escape the idea that he was the puppet master. It was time to come out of softly-softly mode and get onto the front foot. Martha knew she couldn't do it herself, not with a major investigation to run, but she also knew exactly who she needed to talk to. Saying goodbye to the chief inspector, she fired off a text to Harry. They needed to speak — urgently.

CHAPTER 13

It was a sight to warm the coldest of hearts. The giant Julie strolling along holding hands with her new wards, Tom and Amelia. Alongside their huge minder they seemed like even smaller versions of themselves. The pair had both been at after-school club, which meant they were a little later than normal. The children were happily chatting away. She might have looked intimidating to most adults, but children adored her.

Their mother and father were waiting by the front door, doing their best to hide the unbridled relief they felt at seeing their children safe.

Martha, who'd timed her arrival to catch Julie, quietly observed it all. She'd stayed nearby to help with the door-to-door, but if she was honest, she was anxious to be close because she couldn't shake the feeling that something else was about to happen. As the family disappeared from view, she filled Julie in on developments.

"A fake bomb, made with gunpowder? That's sending a pretty weird message," said Julie. "What's your theory?"

"Two-fold," said Martha. "Partly it's a way of keeping everyone on edge. A sort of 'we can get you anytime' type of thing. But I also wonder if it's a distraction. They'd know we have to react to it, and that would mean sealing off the area and bringing in the bomb squad."

"Ooh!" said Julie, her hand going to her mouth. "I need to tell you something in case you hadn't heard. This only happened in the last few hours, but do you know about the odd accident today, involving a mother who lives near here? Fancy house, rich husband."

Martha went very still as she fixed her friend with an intense stare.

"I'll take that as a no then," said Julie. "OK. I stress this isn't from the horse's mouth but from one of the parents at the school. We were talking while waiting for the kids."

"Can we skip the background and get to it?" said Martha, who was unusually terse.

"Easy tiger, you'd be the first to complain if I didn't give you any context," said Julie. "Here's what I've been told. Seems they found the woman in the back garden with severe head injuries. First thoughts are that she may have fallen out of her bedroom window."

"What's the woman's name?" Martha's tone was urgent. "And where does she live?" Julie's shrug and shake of the head left her fighting to contain her frustration. If it was thought to be simply a tragic accident, she wouldn't have been informed about it as a matter of urgency. Bureaucratic procedures were an endless source of irritation.

Martha pulled her mobile out of her pocket and called the chief inspector, but his phone went to voicemail. She left a message then called Krisha, who promised to get on it. "I'm only a short walk away. Hopefully I'll have something by the time I get to you."

As good as her word, Krisha walked into view a few moments later, her phone glued to her right ear. Martha fought the urge to interrupt. Oblivious to the attention focused her way, she carried on her conversation. "So that's Nightingale, as in the nurse?" She listened for a few more seconds then ended the call, nodded at Julie and pointed over Martha's shoulder.

"The house is that way, not far from here but out of sight. The victim's name is a Maria Nightingale. She was pronounced dead at the scene and taken straight to the nearest hospital, King's College."

"Any update on what happened?" asked Julie.

"No, not yet, but we are expecting one very soon. Police are at the scene," said Krisha.

"In that case, lead the way," said Martha. She forced herself to keep calm. She didn't know yet if this was linked to her case — maybe it was a tragic accident. But maybe it wasn't. She took a deep breath. It's tough fighting paranoia when you know there *are* people out to get you.

As Martha made to move, her phone started ringing. It was Tony. She filled him in on what they had, and he sighed. "Sounds like left hand, right hand. I'll bet my sergeant assigned an officer to it while I was in meetings. I blame myself; I should have flagged up that you needed to hear about anything that happened in the area. I'll get that sorted out right now and get back to you."

Martha stared intently at her phone. It was too easy to see enemies everywhere she looked and just as easy to imagine he was part of a conspiracy. If she went down that rabbit hole, it would be a disaster. She needed to stick to her instincts and trust in Tony. He was a good man who had sounded genuinely annoyed.

She knew she had spent a bit too long in her own thoughts when she became aware that Krisha was looking at her quizzically. Martha rolled her shoulders like a boxer in a fight and indicated Krisha take the lead as they set off at a brisk pace, arriving at a detached house painted white and sitting on a generous corner plot. As they stepped closer, Tony rang back.

"First thing to tell you is we've got lucky. It's being handled by Detective Constable Sally Thomas. She's one of the best. She'll help you."

Martha ended the call then looked at Krisha. "Do you know a DC Thomas?"

"I don't really know her, but I hear she's alright. Is that who they've sent?"

Before she could answer a young woman with dark brown hair swept out of the house. As she walked towards them Martha noted she was a similar build to herself, just a couple of inches shorter. She was wearing a grey jacket, black trousers and a white T-shirt and looked, Martha thought, like she belonged. She drew up close enough to Martha to make her feel uncomfortable and stood there eyeballing her.

"So, you're the wet-behind-the-ears bitch that reckons she can take my murder case off me?"

CHAPTER 14

Imelda Taylor yelped as she punched the kitchen wall in frustration. She and her mother had spent the morning locked in the most intense argument they'd ever had.

Her blood pumping from the murder of Maria Nightingale, Imelda had been awake all night replaying her triumph. She'd created a highlights reel in her head which allowed her to watch over and over again as the inebriated Maria disappeared out of the window. She thought the best bit was watching her feet slide over the window ledge followed by a wet crunching sound, although that last bit might have been wishful thinking.

Still awake and hyper, she'd gone out at 6 a.m. to pick up a bag of pastries for Audrey's breakfast. Her mother was partial to a cinnamon whirl — three, to be exact. She even decided to have one herself. Today was going to be a red-letter day, once breakfast was out of the way.

The plan seemed simple at first. Audrey started out in a conciliatory mood and had complimented Imelda on the success of the killing. She'd been checking the news sites, she said, adding, "You did well, and so far, it seems the police are treating it as an accident. That may not last, so enjoy it for now."

Emboldened, Imelda decided now was the right time to reveal the details of her new plan. "I want to bring the schedule forward. Let's do the next one today."

Audrey reacted instantly, shouting, "No!" at the top of her voice.

But Imelda wasn't going to give in without a fight.

"Not being rude, but you just sit here while I go out and do all the hard work. I'm telling you we need to pick things up, move faster. That way the coppers will be running about without the faintest idea of what's really going on."

Audrey's rage was obvious. "You stupid girl! What makes you think you know best? There's a plan and we don't want to change it."

Imelda stuck her nose in the air. "Plan, plan, plan. Who cares about the plan? I don't. I want to kill some rich bitch."

Audrey had turned a very dark purple. She was sweating heavily and complained about chest pains. She waved a feeble hand at her daughter. "You can't go against the plan, you just can't." Beneath the bluster Imelda detected a touch of anxiety in her mother's voice.

Despite her own bubbling anger, this gave Imelda pause. Her mother seemed unusually set on this plan, as if it were something which couldn't be challenged. Before she could press for more information, her mother launched a self-pitying missile.

"Your foolishness will be the death of me, girl. I need rest, help me to my bedroom." She was slumped back in her chair, unmoving.

Imelda took one look and decided her mother could stay where she was. She was far too heavy to haul into the bedroom, not for Imelda on her own, and it didn't look like Mummy was going to be any help at all. She'd injure both of them.

Imelda unwisely tried to ease the tension by punching the kitchen wall. As she blew on her bruised knuckles she glared at her mother. Her only consolation was that while Audrey was asleep, at least she wasn't shouting. In fact, it was blessedly quiet, no rumbling snoring to disturb the peace.

CHAPTER 15

"What? What's going on? Did you say murder? Are you Detective Constable Thomas? I thought this death was being treated as a tragic accident."

Martha was embarrassed at the way she blurted out a series of questions. This woman had completely thrown her off balance, not least by claiming this was a murder. Sally stared at Martha a moment longer before her fierce expression morphed into a face-splitting grin.

"I'm sorry, I couldn't resist," said Sally. "You should see your faces; you both look like you're sucking on lemons." Her eyes, which matched the colour of her hair, were filled with mischief.

A bewildered Martha was struggling to understand what was going on. Her furrowed brow caught Sally's attention, who stopped laughing and wiped her eyes with the back of her hand.

"Give me a minute. I know my sense of humour doesn't always work on everyone, but I was joking, I assure you. To answer one question, yes, I'm DC Thomas."

Martha blinked rapidly. "You certainly had me going there, and Krisha, too, judging by the way she's giving you the eyes."

Far from being abashed, the detective laughed again and then waited for them both to suit up before taking them to where the body had been found. "Let me show you what we're looking at and tell you one of the reasons I'm suspicious," said Sally. Her manner was now all business, no trace of the prankster who had met them. It was like being with a different woman.

She led the pair round the back of the house. The garden was south-facing, and it was hot and sunny. Virginia creeper grew up the walls and framed an open sash window.

"That's the window she appears to have fallen out of . . . judging by where she landed," said Sally, using her index finger to trace how Nightingale had tumbled out of the window, finishing up by pointing out a bloody patch on the patio. Her index finger went back to the upstairs window. "And that's making me suspicious."

Martha followed the direction she was pointing at. "Have you seen something that suggests this was no accident?"

Sally looked at her approvingly. "I have," she said. "From the inside that windowsill is quite high; you'd need to make a big effort to accidently fall out of it. And Maria Nightingale was a smallish woman, about five feet four inches. Plus, the body had marks on one side that could be consistent with Mrs Nightingale being shoved from behind and scraping hard against the wall. I know it's hardly conclusive, and we need the CSIs to work their magic, but I think we need to consider the possibility that she was murdered, at least until the evidence points us either way."

"Before we go down that path, is there anything that could point to a different conclusion? Doesn't an accident sound the most likely answer?" asked Martha.

"Can't rule it out," admitted Sally. "I should have mentioned there was an almost cloying smell coming off the body, most likely alcohol, and we found pills and what is almost certainly vodka in her room — which to me had all the hallmarks of a drunk trying to keep her habit secret." Sally held up both hands. "I get it. Everything I've said could work for a verdict of self-harm, or even a tragic accident. But those marks on her body are very extensive. Did she get those because she was pushed?"

Martha puffed her cheeks. "Something very odd is going on. We started looking at a nothing case about cats and that grew into death threats and bomb scares. Now we have this death to add to the mix — and we all know what we think about coincidences. My guess is that it's all linked."

Sally looked at Martha, her gaze unreadable. Then she nodded once as if she'd made a decision. "I've got a confession to make."

Martha raised an eyebrow but said nothing.

"I've been working on a very complex fraud case. It started eighteen months ago and mushroomed. It's all starting to fall into place, and I'd like to get back to it because we're on the brink of making arrests. It's been my life for quite a while.

"I only got put on this case because I made the mistake of walking past the duty sergeant just as he needed to assign someone. So here I am." She sucked in air through her teeth and carried on. "How about this for a plan? I get back to my fraud case but I'm on call for you if you think you need me."

"Give me a minute," Martha told Sally before taking Krisha to one side. "How would you react if I put you up for a promotion? It can only be temporary for now but how does 'acting detective' sound? If I can get promoted to head bottle-washer, I'm going to need a right-hand woman."

"That would mean a lot to me," said Krisha, who seemed to stand an inch taller. "I won't let you down."

"I know you won't," said Martha, and turned back to Sally. "OK, you hand over everything you have to us, and we take it from there. But it would be great to have you on the end of a phone, as it were."

"That's great," replied Sally. "My fraud case is so close that I'd hate to see someone else step in and take the credit. There's not a lot else I need to add. My next two tasks were organising a CCTV hunt and talking to the husband. I've left him in the kitchen and told him to go nowhere apart from the loo."

"Any other family?" asked Martha.

"Two sons at boarding school, the victim's mother lives in Cumbria so will also be down tomorrow. The husband is an only child, and both his parents are dead."

"I guess we have to consider the husband as a suspect, at least for now," said Martha. "Although, if this does turn out to be a domestic, I'll need to reconsider my brilliant theory."

"Not just yet, Holmes," said Sally, wagging a finger at her. "According to Mr Nightingale he was locked in an all-day meeting at Canary Wharf with thirty other people. Claims the only time he got out was to go to the loo and he was in the meeting when we contacted him. I managed to get that out of him."

"Sounds like a strong alibi," said Martha.

"He's given me a couple of names to check with. I've got calls in and should be hearing back at any moment. Shall I hand this on to Krisha?"

"Please do," said Martha. "What about the CSI team here? Have they said anything yet?"

As she spoke a white-suited figure walked into view. "That's the lead CSI," said Sally, waving at the man. "We were just talking about you, Dave. Please meet Martha, she's the senior officer on this case and that's Krisha who's working with her."

David Drinkwater grunted in a non-committal way. The only bit of him Martha could make out were his light-blue eyes, which now settled on her. He wasn't smiling.

"Let me guess: it's very urgent. Have I got a cause of death? Was it murder? Is there any evidence that identifies the killer? Have the blood tests come back yet? That should cover the key questions," said the CSI. "Right now, the answer to each question is 'yes, no, maybe and no'."

"Actually, there's one thing you've missed out," said Martha. "I need to know the winning numbers for tomorrow night's national lottery."

Martha could tell Drinkwater was smiling now because it touched his eyes.

"As soon as I know the answers to your professional questions you will be told," said Drinkwater. "You might be waiting a long time for the lottery numbers."

Martha resisted replying. She felt the CSI had something on his mind and sensed that he wasn't entirely confident about saying what it was. If she distracted him now, he would keep his thoughts to himself — at least until he was sure about what he had.

He sighed. "I share your view that the victim may have been drinking. There was a glass on the table by her bed which smelled of alcohol, most likely vodka. I also found several packets of codeine tablets on the side. Booze and codeine would be a pretty toxic combination. I got here while the paramedics were still working on her. They said her pupils were down to pinpricks.

"There's one other thing, and I stress this is not conclusive, but more interesting was what I found by the window."

He had Martha's full attention.

"The carpet in that room is cream coloured and good quality with a soft, deep pile. By the window are two faint impressions of the tips of a pair of shoes. Mrs Nightingale was barefoot."

"Could that mean someone was behind her?" said Martha.

"That's exactly what I'm thinking. Only a guess, but I think there was someone else in that bedroom."

"Could you tell if it was a male or female footprint?" asked Martha.

"I'm afraid not. My guess would be male, but I could easily be wrong. It's only a partial footprint — it won't give me any idea of shoe size or what the tread was like. I've got quite a bit of work to do back at the lab before I can be certain. The computer may give us more detail once we've done a really intensive check."

Martha was glad she'd trusted her instincts and waited.

Sally's phone rang. She spoke briefly then asked the caller to hold on.

"I need to pass you to a colleague," she said, then held her mobile towards Krisha. "It's one of the people at the meeting with the husband today."

Krisha listened and asked a question before ending the call saying, "Thank you for that. It's really helpful. Are you there tomorrow? We'd like to get a statement off you. Nothing to worry about, purely routine."

She handed the phone back to Sally. "That's interesting. The husband was there but disappeared for about half an hour after lunch, maybe forty-five minutes."

"I've lived in Dulwich all my life. I've made that journey loads of times, by car, running, cycling — you name it," said Martha. "It would have to be first thing on a Sunday morning with clear roads to do it that fast. I can't see it."

"I agree, it would take a miracle. The only thing is, the guy I spoke to was a bit vague on timings. Maybe it was longer. Let's say Nightingale was really missing for an hour. That's still tight, but a bit more possible."

"Good point," said Martha. "Stay on it and get that time frame pinned down. Let me know the moment you do."

Martha switched to Sally.

"Is now a good time to let you get back to your other job? I'll bring the chief inspector up to speed. He's been pretty supportive so far."

Sally nodded and they shook hands. Martha called over to Krisha. "Shall we go and talk to the husband?"

CHAPTER 16

Stewart Nightingale 'confessed' the moment the two detectives walked into the kitchen. He was sitting at an oak table that was big enough for ten people, staring at a nearly full bottle of beer.

"This is my fault. I knew what was happening, the drink and the painkillers, and I should have done more to help her. But by the time I realised what was going on, it was too late to save our marriage. And I found someone else."

He paused, nervously chewing at his bottom lip. "I lied earlier on when I said I never left my meeting. I sneaked out to see my girlfriend."

Krisha was sitting quietly as Martha took the lead. "It would be very helpful if you started at the beginning. Tell us where you were and exactly what you were doing between 10 a.m. and 3 p.m. today."

Nightingale clenched and unclenched his hands as he looked up. Martha read a range of emotions on his face — contrition, embarrassment and resignation.

"The truth is that Maria hadn't been herself for a while, she'd lost her . . . I'm not sure of the words, but *joie de vivre* probably covers it. Then she had that nasty injury, which opened the door to the drug taking. Maybe this was a way of finding release. I remember reading somewhere that addicts are often tortured souls. That's what makes them seek escape from their demons."

"It sounds like you're claiming your wife may have been suicidal." The interruption came from Krisha, and Martha studied Nightingale's reaction. He blinked rapidly.

"I am being a little melodramatic. I certainly didn't mean to imply suicide."

Martha stole a quick glance at her assistant. The PCSO was diligently taking notes.

Nightingale carried on. "I can say she did try hard to disguise her problems . . ."

Martha was impatient to get on with the details. "Thank you for the background. Now I need you to take your time and be specific about your movements today. We also need to talk to your girlfriend."

This prompted Nightingale to take his phone out of his pocket and scroll through his contacts. "She's called Valerie, Valerie Johnson. Those are all her details." He tapped the screen then passed the phone to Krisha.

"I haven't spoken to her yet," said Nightingale.

"You've told us you were at a meeting today. Can you go through that in detail? When did you leave?" said Martha.

"It was a meeting for the top team, a sort of catch-up on where we are and where we need to be. It started at ten and was over at three," said Nightingale. "I did leave, for almost an hour. I met my girlfriend around lunchtime. I feel so bad about that now. Maybe if I'd been at home Maria would still be here."

Martha couldn't help thinking Nightingale was trying quite hard to win sympathy he didn't deserve.

"Perhaps you're being too hard on yourself. With so many people relying on you it must be very difficult to turn your back on work and go home."

Nightingale couldn't hold back the hint of a smile. "Thank you for your understanding. But I do feel guilty."

Martha pressed on and asked him for the names and numbers of people who could confirm he was in the meeting earlier today. He texted her details of three people then listened quietly as Martha added, "I assume you'll be staying in the house, sir. We may need to ask you some more questions."

They headed for the back garden, where Krisha kicked irritably at the grass. "Typical, he has a sneaky leg-over and then wants the rest of the world to feel sorry for him."

"I agree," said Martha. "The only thing we can do is make sure we check out his story."

Privately she wasn't at all convinced the checks would show anything, but didn't want to deter Krisha. Nightingale was guilty of cheating on his wife and was probably worried about how that news would go down with the people he worked with. But stone-cold killer? She doubted it.

Something occurred to her. "Can you talk to Sally and see if she can do a deep dive on his financials? She is a fraud expert."

"Sure, what are you looking for?" said Krisha.

"I want to be quite sure he didn't pay anyone to kill his wife. Hand on heart, I doubt if he did. He had no need. A nice little life with a girlfriend in tow, and wifey spending all her time stoned."

Martha's phone rang. It was the CSI: she put him on speakerphone, balancing her handset on the palm of her hand.

"I was saying that we got the blood results back. Mrs Nightingale was loaded with codeine. She had six hundred milligrams in her blood; that's about ten times the biggest dose for pain relief."

"Might that be a typical amount for an addict?" asked Martha.

"Maybe. But it's a seriously large dose. It would have a lethal effect on most people. What makes me suspicious is how she ingested such a huge quantity. To my mind it suggests it was disguised in a drink. I'll keep you in close touch."

CHAPTER 17

Imelda nearly jumped out of her skin as her mother's phone sounded. She'd spent the last few hours sitting in silence and the sudden noise gave her a fright. The phone was on the table between them, and she saw the screen said: *Caller ID Withheld*. Probably a spammer, as her mother made no move to answer. The call rang out then started again. Again, Audrey ignored it. On the third ring Imelda impatiently answered.

"Yes. Who is this?"

"Where is Audrey?" said a man.

"She's not available," said Imelda, casting a glance at her mother. The call ended.

She frowned at the phone. The man had acted like he knew Audrey.

Maybe she shouldn't have assumed it was a nuisance caller. She rubbed her eyes in frustration, hard enough to hurt and make her vision swim.

She grabbed the phone, thinking to call back, before berating herself for forgetting that wasn't possible.

She angrily threw herself back in her chair. She needed to think faster. As soon as the man had asked for her mother, she should have done her best to talk to him, offer to take a message or anything to keep him on the phone. Instead, she'd been too abrupt and let him get away.

For the next hour she sat in the gloom as the light slowly faded. She knew her mother was getting help from someone — she hadn't dreamed this plan up all on her own, no matter how hard she tried to make out she had. One part of Imelda thought it would be a good idea to press on alone, another part, quieter but more sensible, knew otherwise.

She was going to have to wait and hope the man called back. The more she thought about it the more obvious it was that he was the brains behind this, if only for one compelling reason: Imelda couldn't remember the last time anyone had called her mother about anything. The fact he had called right at this moment was, to her mind, proof positive.

Just as Imelda was about to call it a day and pour out the evening drinks — Audrey liked to shout at the news after a couple of rounds — her mother's mobile went off again.

Imelda picked it up like it was an unexploded bomb. Her hand was shaking, and she forced herself to speak slowly. "Audrey's phone. Imelda speaking."

She heard the sound of breathing, and as he began to speak, she recognised the man's voice. "I have wanted to talk to you for some time."

"You want to talk to me?" Imelda's voice squeaked with surprise and pleasure. No one ever wanted to talk to her.

"Oh, yes. You obviously have the qualities I'm looking for. I suspect you are a stone-cold killer, one who enjoys murdering people and can be trusted to get the job done."

Most people would have been shocked that anyone, let alone a stranger, would make such a statement. There it was, right out in the open. Imelda was a murderer, a killer, an assassin. But Imelda felt a hot flush of pleasure. This man didn't think she was just some run-of-the-mill woman — and some of that was down to her upbringing. For as long as she could remember her mother had drummed into her that life had been unjust, not giving either of them what they truly deserved. From the age of seven, Audrey had encouraged her little girl to view everyone else as inferior beings, bumps in the road to be negotiated. "Power is for those who take it," Audrey told Imelda. That alone might have produced someone arrogant and unpleasant — but, as her teachers were starting to notice, Imelda was developing sociopathic tendences that saw other children run away rather than risk being trapped by her. By her early teens Imelda was fast on her way to becoming a dangerous young woman.

None of that mattered now as she replayed the man's words. To hear him praising her was a tonic to her dark soul. She beamed with pride. Then a very large thought intruded.

"How can you know something like that about me? We've never even met, let alone spoken."

He laughed, a cold sound without humour. "We have met, when you were a little girl and your mother brought you with her while she cleaned my flat. Even then it was obvious to me that you had something about you, something that marked you out from ordinary people." The voice stopped but she could still hear his breathing, a slow rhythmical sound which calmed her and drowned out all other noise. He spoke again.

"As you got older your mother stopped bringing you so often, but she always talked about you, so much so that I know you as well as I might if you were my own." He laughed again. "Of course, she didn't mean to tell me that you were a killer in waiting. She was very proud of you and thought she was describing a bright young woman who was missing out because she lacked high-level connections. She told me how unfair life was and how the world didn't recognise your special talents. Which I might add you do have, just not the ones Audrey believes." There was the slightest pause. "Did you know she came to me after you announced you wanted a job in publishing? She asked for my help."

Now it was Imelda's turn to laugh. "That's typical of her, always misreading things. I only came up with the suggestion because she kept asking me what I was going to do with myself. Truthfully? I can't see myself getting on with all those hoity-toity book types."

"Since we're being honest, neither could I," came the reply. "But your mum could. She really thought you would enjoy a glittering career as a behind-the-scenes shot-caller. I went along with it, partly because I could see no reason to burst her bubble — but mostly because it suited my purposes to play her along."

He paused and she could hear his breathing again. "I hope you don't mind me being frank. It's not that I think your mum is a fool, but she is blinded by her natural motherly love. She cannot see you as anything but beautiful and talented. You are both those things, but your skills are far from conventional.

"It suited me to go along with Audrey's little conceit since it allowed me to get the ball rolling on my own plans and would, eventually, get me access to you."

Imelda gripped her phone tightly. Now they were getting to it.

"First up, you need to know I'm not giving you any details about me. Especially not my name."

Imelda started to protest but he cut her off.

"That's non-negotiable. Second up, this is what I know about you. Your true personality emerged at your school. By the age of thirteen you were running a very successful extortion racket aimed at your fellow pupils. Your mother, bless her, believes to this day that the money you were awash with was given to you by fellow pupils, grateful for help you gave them with homework.

"That alone was enough to alert me that my suspicions about your special skills were right, and I made inquiries. I discovered that your teachers strongly suspected what you were doing but couldn't get anyone to go on the record. It was said that anyone who broke your code of silence suffered a savage beating."

Imelda was so pleased to have someone to boast to, she couldn't help interrupting. "That place danced to my tune. Once I'd put a couple of snitches in hospital the word got out. I used to batter a few anyway, for the fun of it. I liked it when they bled, and the snot ran out of their noses. I hated the cry-babies, though. Anyone who snivelled really got a slapping."

That cold laugh came again. "Thank you for confirming what I believed to be the case. What about the baby rabbits, though? That was quite a coup you pulled off there. Care to talk me through it?"

Imelda snickered. "I hated those bloody rabbits. The whole school went stupid when the babies arrived. All the kids were smiling and petting them . . . what a bunch of losers. So, I thought, let's teach them a lesson. I killed them and nailed their bodies to a wall in the main hall. Everyone knew it was me, but could they prove it? No chance. I kept smiling, even when I was called in to be questioned by the head. She tried to get all heavy with me, but I ignored her. After that she kept trying to catch me out, but it never worked. Eventually I left to go to college for my A-levels. She was delighted to see me go. I broke in one night and did a shit in her drawer as a thank you. Dozy cow."

The man was laughing again and this time there was warmth in it.

"You're priceless, Imelda, and just what I need for the next stage. If you're in agreement I'd like to tell you what I have in mind." Taking her silence as agreement he outlined his plan. "Keep in mind that I am only going to tell you what you need to get the job done.

"Basically, there is a detective called Martha Munro who's managed to get her nose into my business, and I intend to stop her doing it.

"Your job is to keep the pressure on her. You've done a fabulous job so far and now it's time to push things to the next level. I want my clever little detective so wrapped up in murder, threats and violence she can't tell what day of the week it is."

Imelda had listened closely. "So long as you let me go and kill the next victim, I'm happy. I don't need to know anything else. I'll do a good job for you, and I'm guessing a man like you will always have work for people like me."

"You can be certain of that. And to sweeten the pot, to say thank you for your work, I intend to pay you a million pounds. It will be in an offshore account that only you can access."

Imelda let out a sigh of pleasure. She could get out of this hellhole. Take her mum on a cruise. Life would be great. Even better, the man had agreed the next murder should take place tonight.

"Our latest victim doesn't fit the pattern in any way," said the man. "His only connection is that he comes from the same area. It will have our little detective scratching her head as she tries to find a link, wondering what she's missed. By the time she works out there's nothing there, it will be too late.

"Get this right, Imelda, and I may pay you the greatest compliment of all. You will know who I am. Very few people do."

He rang off, leaving Imelda holding the phone. She thought the man was a little over the top, but decided she could forgive that in return for what he offered — keeping her on the path of murder.

CHAPTER 18

At precisely 9 p.m., Geoffrey Renton was walking out of the door of his modern townhouse close to Gypsy Hill rail station. Walking out of the door with him was his fat, elderly, black Labrador, Jasper. There was no need to put the dog on a lead. Even before arthritis had started affecting his joints, Jasper had never been a big walker. But he was a champion sniffer. All he needed was a blade of grass and he was happy until he was nudged into walking at least a few feet to the next blade of grass.

For Renton this meant the so-called walk amounted to little more than waiting in a few different places while the dog lost himself in a world of smells. Not that his owner minded. He used the time to start thinking about the game of bridge he had scheduled for tomorrow. His partner was one of the better players, and he was confident they would do well in the mini tournament.

Man and dog were both so absorbed in their own little worlds that neither responded when a Range Rover parked on the other side of the road coughed into life. It had been stolen that afternoon and dropped off in Brixton for Imelda to collect.

With his mind on the card game, Renton didn't respond as the Range Rover powered towards him. By the time he looked up it was too late. The car smashed into Renton, hurling him back against the wall and flipping him straight over, so that the back of his head smashed into the ground with a sound like wet cement hitting the bottom of a bucket — killing him instantly. By some miracle, Jasper escaped death by a few inches. The car came to a halt amid a cloud of steam. There was complete silence and then Imelda climbed out and looked down at the victim, who was clearly dead, before heading to the nearby rail station. Wearing dark clothes, a hat and glasses, she never looked back. Because Renton was such an exacting timekeeper, she was able to match the attack with the train timetables, and minutes later she was heading for Victoria station, her mind already turning to the next job.

* * *

Tony contacted Martha at 9.30 p.m. "We've got a man killed in a hit-and-run. It's an odd one, so I thought of you."

"Ha, ha," said Martha. "I take it you're thinking this relates to my two murder cases, sir."

"I think we have to consider it."

"You say it was unusual?"

"We have one witness who was apparently looking out of her window at the right moment. She claims the vehicle was parked up, and she was keeping an eye on it because she thought the driver was up to no good, maybe a burglar.

"She was so keen to tell us, that she approached the responding officer immediately and told him it looked like the car had been aimed at the victim, a Geoffrey Renton — he was an accountant, no family, never married and never been in trouble with the police — and our witness says the driver got out, inspected the body, then ran off towards Gypsy Hill station, abandoning his Range Rover, which had been reported stolen a few hours earlier."

Martha thought hard. "It's happened just far enough outside our current zone of investigations to make you wonder if it's a coincidence, but I suspect it's far too close to be anything other than connected. It's got all the hallmarks of the killer we're looking for in the Nightingale case. It feels bold and well planned without having any motive.

"I mean, Maria Nightingale was a tragic woman, but there seems nothing about her that would merit her being singled out in the way she was. And from what you've told me there's nothing about Renton that marks him out."

"Unless the pair of them formed the most unlikely criminal gang ever," said the chief inspector.

"Quite, sir. I suppose I'm going to have to keep an open mind. Maybe this is just some kind of crazy rampage."

"As unlikely as that might be, go where the evidence takes you."

"Agreed, sir. I was already thinking of this as a very sinister investigation, but never in my wildest dreams did I think it would come to this. It makes me worried that there could be a direct attack on the Browns. I'm glad I asked Julie to stay around this evening — on her own she'll deter most attackers. I know a request for armed protection is being processed. I think this may turn out to be another reason why it should happen."

"Whatever happens, I want you on this case and in a senior position. I don't want a DI appointed as SIO, so I have a suggestion of my own. This case needs more firepower. How about I nominally take charge but you remain the SIO on the ground. You could be my deputy, with the rank of acting inspector. It's a huge jump for you, but you've demonstrated outstanding detective skills so far. I don't want to lose your input just as everything comes to the boil. I'm also drafting in an outstanding officer, Detective Sergeant Gill Harrison, to run the minutia of the incident room; she'll sort out the manpower needed for building up profiles, that leaves you free to focus on the detecting. If you could send me an email outlining who's done what so far, that will make sure we stay in control."

Martha was initially speechless, finally managing to reply, "Thank you, sir. I hope I don't let you down. As you may have heard, Sally is going back to her fraud case, and I've asked Krisha to step up. I really think she can handle it, but she also knows the final decision lies with you."

He didn't hesitate. "I'm more than happy with that arrangement. DC Thomas has worked wonders on her case and needs to see it through. Carry on and I'll clear it with the top brass." He thought for a second. "I'm thinking it might help if I have a quick chat with Krisha, to offer my full support, make sure she knows we're all behind her and she's got this promotion on merit."

"That would be great," said Martha. "If fifteen minutes is enough, why not grab her after our early briefing tomorrow?"

"Perfect, fifteen minutes will be more than enough," said Tony.

CHAPTER 19

The hit-and-run witness turned out to be a white-haired old lady with a face covered in wrinkles and a mind like a steel trap. Maisy Leake, a widow, was currently standing by the window in her front room as she showed Martha how she'd kept the Range Rover driver under observation.

"She turned up just after eight o'clock and just sat there. She had a cap on, but I know it was a woman. I didn't like the look of her, so as there was the usual rubbish on the telly, I thought I'd watch her instead.

"I turned my lights off so she couldn't see me. She kept looking down and I guessed she was checking the time.

"It all happened really fast. Mr Renton came out with Jasper to get some air. He's as regular as clockwork. They stopped so Jasper could have a sniff — he could sniff for Britain, that dog — and a few seconds later it was all over. The car shot across the road and hit Mr Renton. He didn't have a chance.

"The driver got out and looked at him. Then there was an odd bit. She seemed to have a conversation with someone, kept pausing like she was listening. Took one more look at the body, then she was gone."

"Just for the record," said Martha, who was impressed by the detailed recall. "You don't think this was an accident."

"No way at all," said Mrs Leake. "Her attention was fixed on Mr Renton the moment he got outside, and she wasn't bothered about what she'd done. If it was an accident, she would have been going mad with anxiety."

"Could you help us with a description?" asked Martha.

"I can, but it might not be much help. She was dressed in big glasses and that cap which hid her features. I can say she was the same height as the car. When she got out, the top of her head was level with the roof."

Martha stayed on the scene until midnight and then figured she needed to go home and get some sleep. She'd already spoken to Krisha at home. She'd wanted to come to the scene, but Martha knew tomorrow would be frantic. "Get some sleep. We start at six in the morning back at the Nightingales'."

* * *

The front of Martha's house was in darkness apart from a faint light from the kitchen at the rear of the terraced property, a Victorian cottage dating back to the 1850s. Her eyes widened. Before she'd been called out to the hit-and-run, she was supposed to be talking to Harry.

Letting herself in, she hurried to the back of the house, where she was pleased to see the familiar sight of Harry sitting at the kitchen table. As always, he was smartly dressed and looked far younger than his official seventy-five years. His appearance was helped by his formidable exercise routine. He could outrun Martha, despite giving away fifty years in age. To emphasise the point, Martha was in top shape herself since Harry acted as her fitness trainer, specialising in self-defence and boxing. He claimed that Martha, who was proud of her powerful shoulders, was one of the better punchers he had come across. While she lacked the brute force of a heavyweight, as a middleweight she was right up there. On one late-night walk she'd put that skill to good use as she dealt with a man who'd made the mistake of thinking she was a victim.

"Harry, I'm so sorry. It's been frantic," said Martha. She'd even forgotten he was babysitting while Julie focused on her guarding job.

"No worries. I played with Betty for a while, she had about a million questions about life, as usual, then she went to bed and has been sound asleep since just after eight," said Harry.

He offered to make her tea, but all she wanted was a long bath and several hours' sleep. But that was a luxury she couldn't afford right now. Even though tomorrow promised to be another long day of police work, she needed to talk to Harry right now. His special skills, contacts and grounded common sense were going to be crucial. Her instincts told her this was the moment she needed him the most.

Mistaking her silence for wanting to be left alone, he made to stand. "I can come back another time — you go to bed."

"No. I need to tell you this and it won't take long." She took a deep breath. "I think *he's* back."

Harry looked as though his heart had been touched by ice. He had no need to ask who *he* was. Harry was all too aware that a man called Neil Thompson had orchestrated a conspiracy that led to Martha being framed for her mother's murder. Harry treated Martha like the daughter he'd never had, and her being under threat seemed to fill him with an equal mix of fear and rage.

With Thompson's name now out in the open, Martha had clung to the belief that her would-be nemesis would be forced back under the stone he had slithered out from. For a short while she'd dared to dream, especially after months went by without further incident. But now she could feel that self-imposed security being stripped away — just as she was being sucked even deeper into a complex murder investigation. If she hadn't had Harry, a man she literally trusted with her life, she might have had to step away, not just from this case, but the police force as well. In fact, she might well have gone into hiding.

Harry was looking at her anxiously. "If I didn't know better, I'd say you were worried sick."

She made herself sit up straight. Late at night after a long day was an easy time to frighten yourself.

"Sorry, Harry," she said. "I'm cross with myself for leaving it so long to talk to you. The moment I heard that an assistant commissioner was involved in a nothing case about cats, I knew in my heart of hearts that Thompson was involved. I tried to hide the truth out of fear, but that's no excuse." She suddenly teared up, something she never did. "What if my delay proves costly and one of you gets hurt, Betty above all?"

Harry patted her shoulder. "Nothing happens to Betty while I'm around, and we're a tough bunch. We won't roll over easy, especially now you've put us on a war footing."

Martha looked at him and felt some of the tension drain away. He might be seventy-five years old, but as genial as he looked, she knew people didn't spend a long career as a gang-land enforcer without some 'special qualities'. Getting past him would be no easy task. If he cared for her, he absolutely adored Betty.

But even Harry's reassuring presence couldn't quite eliminate all her fears. Harry chose that moment to speak. "I've known you since you were a baby, literally, and you've always been a tough one. But something is bothering you."

She sighed heavily. "There is. I don't know what he can want. As far as I know that woman who was close to my dad, Carol, took the last remaining copy of his diary. I don't have anything else, neither do you. So why is Thompson still after us? Am I missing something?"

Harry shook his head. "Whatever it is at least we know about him."

"That's right, we do know about him!" Martha leaped up, her eyes bright. "I've had a thought. He always likes to work behind the scenes." She paused, staring intently at Harry, who knew her well enough not to interrupt.

"Who has he got on the investigation team? I know about the assistant commissioner and Sergeant Edwards, but they're outside the main circle, as it were." She chewed her lip, feeling like her old self. On the front foot and pushing hard.

"It's not me, obviously, and I'd put my life on Krisha being as straight as they come. I don't see how it could be Sally, she talked herself out of the team almost straight away . . . I hate to say it, but it leaves Tony Green as the number one suspect."

"Leave it up to me," said Harry. "Let me very quietly ask around. If there's something funny about him, I'll hear."

Martha smiled at Harry. He was a man who could be trusted, which was a paradox given his background. His criminal past had left him with a unique range of contacts who between them would hopefully provide vital clues about the enemy.

Harry sat patiently while she tried to put her thoughts in order. Eventually, he broke the silence. "Apart from his name and knowing how powerful he is, we don't really know much about this Neil Thompson. Is he a policeman, like your dad, or maybe something else? Who are the people he works through? He must have trusted wingmen. We certainly don't know what he looks like or even if that's his real name."

Martha said nothing for a moment, before regaining her focus. "You're right, of course. Until recently the only possibility I'd risk my police pension on is that he wasn't in the Old Bill. Now I'm not so sure. Where better to hide than in plain sight? I'm not saying that is an even bigger reason to check Tony Green, but we can't rule anything out." She rubbed her gritty eyes. "Does that make me sound paranoid?"

Harry didn't reply, but sometimes that was the sensible option.

"While you're at it, there's another cop for you to chase down. The sergeant I mentioned, Roger Edwards, he ran the admin for the detective pool," said Martha. "I thought he was burying me with crap. Except, it turns out he was pushing me where Thompson wanted me. He's no criminal mastermind, but maybe he knows enough to help us. Now, he's suddenly vanished — retired, with no send-off. Maybe you can track him down?"

If Martha was worried, then that was enough for Harry. "Leave it with me. I'll make some inquiries, but ultra low-key." Harry quickly made a note. "I'll need to keep an eye on Betty, she's obviously the most vulnerable. Any chance of freeing up Julie?"

Martha blinked as she thought it through. He was right about Betty, and as much as she hated to let the Browns down, Betty was her daughter. There was no competition.

"Let me think it through properly. If you stick with Betty for now, I'll work out the best way we can share out Julie so we can keep everyone safe. It's all linked though, and Betty goes to the same school that Julie is covering, so that helps."

Harry made a fist, which he gently punched into his other hand. "If *that* man is back, we all need to be on top of our game."

He stood up. "Do you mind if I move in for a little while? I can sleep on the sofa, but you can come and go, knowing Betty is safe." Harry didn't wait for an answer, heading out for his home, just a few doors away from Martha's. "I'll be back with my stuff in a jiffy. You go to bed. I'll be quiet as a mouse."

Martha stretched her arms. It was a good feeling to know Harry had her back. Heading upstairs, she had enough energy to brush her teeth before collapsing into bed. Despite being exhausted, sleep proved elusive, with her mind constantly throwing up the same question. Was everything leading up to Neil Thompson making a direct attack on Martha, her daughter or her friends? She had a bad feeling she knew the answer.

CHAPTER 20

It felt like seconds had elapsed as she was dragged from sleep by the pinging of her mobile phone. It was a message from Tony Green, who'd resolved the issue of where to put a mobile incident room by ordering in two. One was currently heading to Gypsy Hill, the other was already in situ in the heart of Dulwich Village. Seeing it was gone 5 a.m., she sprang out of bed and after a quick shower went downstairs to be handed a mug of strong 'builder's tea'. As she took a reviving sip, she decided there was something magical about Harry's brew. It always hit the spot.

"Did you get any sleep on that sofa last night?" Martha asked.

"Don't need it at my age. Besides, I try to avoid getting too much shut-eye. Never know if I'm going to wake up again."

"Comedy and protection in one package," said Martha, snorting with laughter. Harry really was a tonic. She pantomimed stroking her chin as if engaged in deep thought. "I met a charming old lady last night. Sharp as a pin and on her own. Fancy an introduction?"

In answer he went to the front door and opened it, pointing outside. "If you're in charge you don't want to be late."

The quick exchange lifted her spirits. It was going to be a grim day. People talk about the first twenty-four hours after a murder as being vital to catching the killer. Martha didn't object to that theory, but what about two murders and a death threat?

Setting off from home, she started out at a fast pace. This might be the only exercise she got, and she was going to make the most of it. She trotted across the South Circular and almost broke into a jog as she went past an entrance to Dulwich Park. Lost in thought she was surprised to find herself at the incident room. She went in to find Krisha already in place, putting the finishing touches to a map highlighting the murder scenes.

She smiled at Martha. "The chief inspector was really singing your praises just now." She couldn't hide a smile. "He confirmed my new assignment and said he'd made you inspector to boot."

"The inspector bit is only for now," said Martha. "Right, what have you got?"

"I compiled all the CCTV and emailed it to DS Harrison, otherwise I wanted to wait for you."

"OK," said Martha. "Stating the obvious, we have two murders to solve and the threats against the Browns. We need to get moving on Geoffrey Renton. What do we know about him and, importantly, is it right to link his murder to Maria Nightingale and the Browns?"

"I think we have to — until we get evidence that proves otherwise," said Krisha. "All we know at the moment is that he was a widower, wife believed to have died of cancer, a story we're checking. He lived alone with his dog and recently retired as some sort of high-powered lawyer specialising in finance. I'm waiting for details."

"Well, push hard for those. In the meantime, I guess we can make some general observations." Martha stretched her neck. It really had been a short night. She pushed any feeling of tiredness to one side and carried on.

"In my opinion, these two killings have a whiff of organisation about them, but I doubt we're dealing with your typical contract killer. I get the feeling that they're enjoying it and like taking risks. It took nerve to break into Maria Nightingale's house, fill her with drugs and push her out of the window. And Geoffrey Renton was mowed down in the street by a Range Rover whose driver walked off as cool as you like. Neither death was a spur-of-the-moment thing. It was all planned, not least nicking the car. So far, the killer seems to have got lucky and avoided being caught on camera, but my sense is that's as much down to luck as it is judgement. I'm not going to be surprised if a CCTV image shows up very soon.

"Also, what do we think about Stewart Nightingale? He's definitely acting a bit off, but is he a killer? I really doubt it. He's got a decent alibi for his wife, and why would he kill Renton? It makes no sense. We'll keep an eye on him until we know better, but low key. Let's take the point of view that we're looking to rule him out."

Martha switched tack.

"I think we all feel this is linked in some way; we just need to work out how. We need to dig down and see if there is some other connection. Were the victims and their families connected via some joint enterprise? Or was it something a more personal? Did they have a shared interest in . . . I dunno, paintings? A bit unlikely, but hopefully you get my drift."

"One other thing," said Krisha, "I have a message from the chief inspector to pass on. He's managed to get us dedicated technical support so we have someone in the incident room who can deal with mobiles and laptops. That should help to see if there are any links between our people."

"That's good," said Martha, trying to keep her expression neutral. She didn't want Krisha to pick up on her concerns. "We also need to do all the obvious things, like asking Mr Brown and Mr Nightingale if they know of each other or Geoffrey Renton. Dulwich isn't such a big place — they might have bumped into each other."

Martha's expression became more serious. "There's one thing that's been bugging me . . . Mrs Nightingale was fed a cocktail of drink and drugs, and I know it's a cliché, but women are poisoners."

CHAPTER 21

Imelda was so pumped with adrenaline she could barely sit still. Unable to sleep, she was watching the news in the early hours, sitting next to her mother, who hadn't even gone to bed. An advert for breakfast cereal popped up, reminding her how hungry she was.

"I think I'll go to that all-night bakery. Do you fancy anything, Mummy?"

There was a long pause, then Audrey made a soft sighing sound. Imelda assumed she wanted her usual order of a bag of frosted cinnamon rolls and a large latte with three sugars.

Imelda hid her grin. She knew exactly which buttons to press when it came to her mother, and she had one more thing to try out.

"While I'm out, do you think it might be a good idea to have a shower? It really is getting a little musty in here."

Audrey's newly increased bulk made her sweat a lot, and she often showered two or three times a day — to suggest she had an odour problem was the biggest possible insult.

As she skipped out of the flat, she could hear Audrey shouting, "How dare you? I'll have you know I'm perfectly clean. If there's a smell, it's down to you. Anyway, you know I'm ill!"

Returning with the food order, she noted her mother still hadn't moved, although she had that sour look she got when she thought Imelda was failing to show her proper respect. Putting on a bright smile, she dumped the pastries in Audrey's lap. "That should keep you going, Mother. Now — have you calmed down enough for me to talk to you? I could still do with your advice."

Audrey refused to look at her daughter but didn't say no.

It was all Imelda needed as she launched into an account of how she had killed the two victims and was preparing for more.

"I know you wanted me to take my time, but things were going so well." She decided to keep it to herself that she was following the advice of the mystery man. He had urged her to keep up her momentum.

Imelda glanced across at her mother, who was sitting stony faced. Time to try a little flattery.

"I can't tell you how helpful it was that you insisted on me being careful about how I dealt with the cats. I went out and got to know the area properly, checked out the CCTV. I couldn't see it all, but I got most of it. I read somewhere that most of those cameras don't work anyway. I wouldn't have done that without you insisting on me doing the research."

Audrey muttered something that Imelda couldn't quite hear, apart from the word "cats".

"Are you thinking about why he made such a fuss about taking the cats?"

Audrey didn't respond, so she took that as her cue to carry on.

"I've been talking to him about that, and his plan is even cleverer than we thought. He wanted to distract the police. Something to do with winding them up, he said. I'm not sure I would've gone to so much bother."

If her mother was pleased by her comments, she did a good job of concealing it. She appeared to have dozed off. Imelda seized her chance to get a bit of air; it *was* getting quite stuffy in the flat. She cracked open a window and to distract herself started thinking about her next murder, the anticipation filling her with glee.

"Wait till you find out what's going to happen next, Mother. If it all goes to plan it might even make the front pages of the newspapers."

CHAPTER 22

Colin Henderson was another man whose actions you could predict. He owned a large, double-fronted Victorian home in Dulwich Wood Avenue, with a driveway that boasted tall brick stacks on either side of the entranceway. Each day he went for a morning bicycle ride, and on his return, he liked to sit up high, arms down by his side and sweep back onto his driveway. It took some skill as, moving fast, he only had sight of his entrance way at the last moment. It was a bit of fun playing make-believe at winning the Tour De France. It was a fantasy that would kill him.

Had he been less determined to get out and paid more attention to the news, he would have learned that a few hundred yards away, Geoffrey Renton, a man he had never met, had been mowed down by a hit-and-run driver.

With all his attention now focused on his ride, he missed Imelda, walking confidently towards his house, her identity obscured by her hoodie. By the time he was gone from view, Imelda had reached the driveway entrance to his home. She quickly pulled on a pair of multi-layered armoured gloves, then from her backpack pulled out a roll of super-strong razor wire. She carefully looped one end of the wire to the first brick pillar that marked the 'returning' entranceway.

Without hesitation, she quickly looped the other end of line around the opposite pillar and pulled it as tight as her gloved hands would allow. It was done in seconds, and she swiftly moved away. Her shoulders hunched as she imagined the alarm being raised, but all was quiet — no one had seen her. She sauntered across the road and checked her watch. In a little over fifteen minutes Henderson would be returning from his ride on his racing bike. Imelda crossed her fingers and hoped he didn't do anything different today. Not wanting to attract attention, she walked away. She would be back in time to see how well the plan, presented to her by Thompson, had worked. She was impressed by the detail he'd provided, right down to the grooves cut into the pillar to make sure the razor wire was at the right height. With less than a minute to go, Imelda was back, looking on from across the road. As the clock ticked down, she saw Henderson hove into view. He was coming fast, very fast, enjoying the last downhill stretch of his ride. With a clear view ahead, he made the turn for home. The watching Imelda couldn't help but admire the way he manoeuvred without touching the handlebars as he shot towards his driveway, unaware of the tightly bound wire. Looking on, Imelda held her breath and was rewarded with a perfect view as the line severed his head, quickly and efficiently. With his heart pumping hard from the ride, blood fountained into the air as the headless corpse continued along the driveway.

At this point his wife opened the front door, a warm smile already forming as she prepared to greet her ever-reliable husband. Instead, she was met with a sight that would haunt her for the rest of her life. As the bike stayed on course for the front door it got close enough for the gushing blood to coat her in its warm, sticky liquid.

The horror was compounded as the head's momentum kept it rolling right up to where she was standing. As she looked down into the familiar blue eyes, she screamed.

CHAPTER 23

Krisha nearly dropped her phone as she heard the inhuman sound. She was a couple of hundred meters away, but the awful keening instantly filled her with dread. She ran towards the source of the terrible noise. Powered by adrenaline, she covered the distance in less than thirty seconds to find the blood-soaked widow standing motionless with her arms by her sides and her face a mask of pain and anguish. Her gaze locked on an object at her feet.

At first Krisha couldn't make out what was holding the woman's attention, then her brain finally accepted the images her eyes were sending. She almost sat down in shock as she first took in the severed head, then the body tangled up with the bike.

Krisha had stopped short of the entrance, pausing as something caught her eye. There was a line stretched between the pillars, something she might have missed were it not coated in gore. She staggered slightly as she made the connection but was quickly back on track. She needed to protect the crime scene and make sure no one else came into contact with the line. She slipped off her high-viz jacket and draped it over the wire. It would have to do and at least everyone would see it.

Meanwhile the woman had stopped screaming and had bent down to pick up the head lying at her feet, then cradled it tightly in her arms as she sat down on the ground. As Krisha got closer the woman looked up, her eyes filled with despair.

With trembling hands Krisha called 999, gave them the details and then called Martha.

"Have you got something?" said Martha, eager for information.

Krisha had to swallow hard against the bile that was burning the back of her throat.

"Yes. But not in the way you were hoping. The killer's struck again," she said.

Clearly it wasn't the news Martha had been anticipating. "Are you telling me we have a third murder . . . what's going on?"

Krisha did her best to make sense of what had happened and report what she could see with her own eyes.

"I'm standing in the driveway of a large house. Lying on the right-hand side of the driveway is a headless body. Sitting on the steps of the doorway is a woman who I believe to be the wife of the victim. She's holding his severed head. I believe this has happened within the last few minutes. I've noticed a thin line stretched between two posts on either side of the entrance. I think this may be how our victim was killed. There's no obvious sign of any other murder weapon." She told Martha the address then swallowed hard again. "I should add that I don't actually know this is a murder, but . . . what else could it be? This is no weird accident."

"My God!" Martha managed. "I'm on the way."

Ending the call, Krisha looked across at the widow, who was sitting on the ground. She looked catatonic, staring down at her husband's head. Krisha wanted to take the woman in her arms, hold her tight. An effort of will slowed her breathing down. She had to act: she couldn't shut down. She worried that her actions might be making things worse but how much worse could it be? She reached out and gently patted the woman on the arm.

She did the best thing she could: guard the scene, and guard the victim's wife. She heard the approach of her boss long before she saw her as Martha arrived in a marked car with lights flashing and siren wailing.

Martha jumped out of the car, heading towards Krisha, who held up a warning hand and pointed at the wire. The blood drained out of Martha's face as she looked around. It was one thing to be told, another to see it. Krisha watched her focusing hard on the details, absorbing what she could see.

Emboldened by the police car's arrival, neighbours started to appear, and one man made to walk up the driveway.

"Stop there. You can't come any further, this is a crime scene!" said Martha, speaking very loudly.

He stood shifting from foot to foot, and she wondered if he was going to ignore her. The uniformed officer who had driven them was out of his car now and heading towards the man. To Krisha everything seemed to be moving in slow motion and she feared the worst, but the man stopped and spoke, his voice a plea.

"Deidre and Colin Henderson are my friends. My wife and I have known them for more than forty years. I need to help her," said the neighbour.

"Your help will be vital," said Martha, "but right now I have to protect this crime scene. We don't want to do anything that might compromise it." She reached out and touched his arm. "Perhaps Mrs Henderson could come to your home? It would be better if we get her away from here. What's your name, sir?"

"I'm Paul Smith and my wife is Anne. Of course Deidre can come. I'll wait, shall I? I need to talk to you anyway. I think I know who the killer is."

Martha looked at Krisha, who had to stop herself running up to the neighbour and shaking him.

CHAPTER 24

Before Krisha could do anything more, a paramedic arrived, along with two more squad cars.

The paramedic sized up the situation and focused his attention on Mrs Henderson — the living came first. He knelt down in front of her, ignoring what she was cradling in her arms as he quickly checked her for signs of injury.

"I can't see any physical damage, although . . ." He trailed off as both he and Martha looked at the head she was cradling in her arms.

The paramedic produced a small blanket from a bag he was carrying, which he suggested Mrs Henderson might like to use to cover her husband's head.

"No. Don't touch him. No one should touch him. I've got to look after him." She spoke fiercely as if daring anyone to say otherwise.

The paramedic gently persisted. "I know this is hard, but would your husband want people to see him like that?"

The paramedic's words got through and Mrs Henderson sagged. She allowed him to take the remains of her husband. He kept up a constant flow of reassurance before suggesting she go inside. He looked at Martha. "Where are we going?"

"We can take her next door. The neighbour is an old friend," said Martha.

"Are you able to walk?" asked the paramedic.

Mrs Henderson whispered something Martha couldn't hear. "That's good, we'll give it a go," the paramedic said before glancing at Martha again. "Are you up to helping? Get round the other side and let her hold on to you if she needs any extra support. I'll take her weight."

Slowly they helped her to her feet, Mrs Henderson laying her arm on top of Martha's with a touch as light as a feather, then they carefully walked towards Mr Smith, who was standing on the pavement, making a huge effort to stay where he was. The paramedic kept the little convoy moving and soon they were walking up to the house next door, where Anne Smith was waiting in the doorway to guide them into a room filled with overstuffed armchairs and settees.

They sat Mrs Henderson down, and Smith started to fuss over his neighbour. Martha deftly stepped up and diverted him, speaking quickly. "You said you know who the killer is."

The neighbour appeared to be in a trance. "What? Oh . . . yes, I did. Sorry, this is almost too much to bear. I can't get my thoughts to work properly."

"That's quite understandable, please don't worry. I can do this after you've had a chance to settle, but is there anything I need to know straight away? Maybe something we need to act on," said Martha.

Smith watched as his wife walked up to Mrs Henderson then turned to Martha. Now he looked less sure of himself. "When I say I know who the killer is . . . well, that is a bit of an exaggeration. But I did see something a bit odd."

He was lost in thought for a moment and Martha gently gripped his forearm. "What did you see, Mr Smith? Just tell me and let us establish how important the information is."

He shook himself. "Yes, yes. Of course. It was a woman, a young woman, I think, although she was wearing one of those hoodies on the two occasions I saw her."

"Two?" Martha's tone was urgent. Could this be the vital breakthrough?

"I'm quite sure I saw her twice. The first time she was near the driveway just after Colin would have left for his bike ride. I was getting my spare glasses from the car and walking back into the house at the time."

"Was she acting in a way that you thought suspicious?"

"Not really. I mean, I didn't see anything that made me think she was up to no good." He was becoming defensive at not having more to go on. Martha quickly moved him on before he started second-guessing himself. He'd seen something and she needed to know what that was.

"You're doing a great job, Mr Smith. Please carry on and tell me about the second time you saw her."

"It was after I heard the screaming. I couldn't make sense of it at first and I was looking out of the window. I saw the policewoman race past towards Colin and Deidre's home. I waited a moment, not sure what to do for the best. It was silly really, but I was shocked, I think, and fearing the worst . . . It was far worse than I could have imagined." He stopped and the faraway look appeared again.

Martha leaned forward and placed her hands on his shoulders, waiting until he looked up and made eye contact.

"What you've seen is beyond imagining, but I need to get hold of who did this. Maybe you have the key to that, maybe you don't. But I do need you to tell me when you next saw this person."

He exhaled sharply like he'd been holding his breath. "It was after the police lady arrived, the one I mentioned earlier. By then my wife asked me to go and see what was going on. That's when I saw her again. I'm sure it was a her, just for a moment.

"I have to admit that my mind was in overdrive, but I'm sure it was the same woman. She was on the other side of the road, looking across. Then she walked away. I remember thinking, who could leave a scene like that?"

"You're sure it was the same person, and you're sure it was a woman?" Martha was making a concerted effort not to shout.

He focused on Martha. "I think so. I really do. She was about your size. I remember thinking she looked like an athlete, like you. But she was definitely wearing the same top, I especially remember the hood."

"You've done really well," said Martha. "Do you recall the colour of the hoodie this woman was wearing?"

"It was a grey colour. I'm quite sure of that. Don't ask me what brand it was though."

"Anything else jump out at you?"

He shook his head then stopped. "She was wearing a pair of bulky orange gloves. Like something you'd wear to protect your hands from extreme heat."

"Could you see any writing on them?" asked Martha, sure he was describing protective gloves that would have allowed her to pull the wire tight.

"I'm sorry, my eyes aren't up to spotting that sort of detail. Anyway, why would she need gloves?" He went very pale, and his mouth opened as he whispered, "Oh."

"Thank you," said Martha. "We need to get a proper statement from you shortly, so someone will come and speak to you."

He nodded, and she noted how shocked he looked. That was the thing about sudden, violent death — the ripple effect of the murder spread over a wide area. She gave him a sympathetic nod and then made a phone call to Tony.

He answered on the second ring.

"I hear we have another killing."

"Yes, sir, we do, and very gruesome. A cyclist has been decapitated — possibly with razor wire — as he cycled into his own driveway."

He breathed in sharply. "My God! Anything we can go on yet?"

"We have a credible report from a neighbour that a young woman wearing a grey hoodie and orange gloves may have been responsible. This has only just happened, so it might be worth putting out an alert."

"On it . . . young woman wearing a grey hoodie doesn't narrow things down much — the gloves help," he acknowledged. "But if she has any sense they'll have been thrown away."

Martha, now back outside, looked around. There was quite a crowd of emergency responders turning up. Even the fire brigade for some reason, probably a result of a panicking 999 operator throwing everything at the call out. At least someone had placed a couple of blankets over the remains. It would keep them hidden until the CSIs got there with their protective tent and the body could be taken away. The last thing she wanted was a picture of the scene turning up on social media. She silently rebuked herself for only just thinking about it. She was in charge, at least right now, and didn't want to give the impression she was being overwhelmed. But this series of killings was going to take every ounce of policing skills she possessed — would it be enough? Maybe it was time she stepped aside as acting inspector.

CHAPTER 25

The chief inspector listened impassively as Martha told him her concerns after he arrived at the latest crime scene.

"I lack experience, and it worries me that I might let you down. You've been so supportive, I'm desperate to prove you right. Not just that, I've been talking to family and friends of the victims. They've got their trust invested in us."

As she finished talking Tony took off his peaked cap, gently smoothing his hair. Martha, fighting an urge to shuffle from one foot to another, was surprised when he laughed, a gentle, good-natured sound that made her relax.

"Not good enough?" he said. "First of all, you owe me nothing. I'm backing you because you have the ability and training. As to you being anxious, so you should be. There's not a detective I know who would be feeling totally confident right now."

He looked around at all the activity, seeming to take careful note of everything he could see.

"This isn't just a serial killer on the loose," he said. "It's a murderous rampage. I think you're coping admirably. I certainly need to assign more resources to you, but that's no reflection on your abilities, quite the opposite. As to your question about whether you're the right person to be running the show, I've got some interesting news. I've just spoken to the commissioner, and she wants her deputy to act as the 'face' of the investigation. Which is good news, since it means you and I focus on the police work and leave media relations to the bosses. We have Deputy Commissioner Roger Croxford to handle all that, and having him on board means no more delays in getting personnel. Even better, the package includes Croxford's right-hand man, Chief Superintendent Alun Williams, a top thieftaker and a top man to boot. He'll be around checking on progress, kicking arses as necessary. He's a real details man who can only help keep the investigation on track.

"I've had a quick word with Croxford already and he commented on what a tight investigation you're running. He wants you to carry on with what you're doing. You keep reporting to me, and I'll liaise with Croxford and Williams. I know this might seem like you do all the heavy lifting while others take the credit, but the right people will know what you're doing."

Martha felt a huge sense of relief. Her biggest fear was being removed from the case altogether, but they were keeping her in place and adding in some real firepower. She wished her parents were alive to see . . . they'd have been proud of her, she was sure.

Tony carried on. "You can expect to see lots of Roger Croxford on TV. The commissioner says this sort of case is catnip for the media, and we'll see all the rent-a-quote politicians pushing the line that London's becoming lawless."

Just then, a police liaison officer arrived to ask Martha if she had any particular instructions.

"Just get alongside the widow for now. She's holding up well, all things considered, but that's not going to last. The paramedics have had a look at her, but we need a doctor as well."

The liaison officer, a friendly looking woman in her forties, was briskly confident. "I'll look out for her, and we can talk again when you're ready."

Tony and Martha watched her walk away. "Sorry, sir, you were talking about the media . . ."

"Yes, and I wanted to add that the moves by the commissioner aren't just window dressing. She's giving us all the resources we could want.

"I've also learned something," he continued, his right eyebrow arching. "You're the legendary John Munro's daughter. If you're half as good as your dad, you'll be very good indeed."

"Thank you, sir," said Martha who could do nothing to prevent her cheeks turning pink. "I wasn't trying to keep it from you, I've just got in the habit of not mentioning my dad."

"Oh, don't worry. I wasn't complaining. My dad was in the Old Bill, not as illustrious as your father, but a detective inspector nonetheless. I've discovered there are some people around who didn't like him. I gather the same could be said for you and your dad."

Martha wasn't sure of the best way to respond. It was strange to be talking to him like this while just a few hours ago she'd told Harry he was a top suspect. She made a note to tell Harry he was the son of a police officer — maybe there was something there.

Tony was looking at her intently, so she switched subjects. "We have another witness who adds to the idea that we're looking for a woman. Krisha has found a reasonable picture on CCTV near the Nightingale home, and I think we get it out to the media as soon as we can. I feel confident that someone will ID her from the picture."

They were briefly distracted as the forensics team took down the wire, which allowed an ambulance to back up the driveway so the body could be moved.

"That sounds like a good plan," said Tony, who was listening closely. "But I do think we stress that this is about needing to eliminate someone from our inquiries. I know you're convinced this is a woman, but we tread lightly. Any misstep on our part will bring down a ton of the smelly stuff."

Martha knew Tony was talking sense. The last thing she wanted was to be accused of missing a key clue because she was obsessing over unproven theories, although she thought he was being quite determined to make his point. She shrugged the thought aside. He was a senior and experienced officer giving her hard-won advice, and she had already warned herself to be cautious in reaching conclusions.

"Don't lose sight of the fact that good old-fashioned police work has got you a long way," said Tony. "You need to throw more people at the door-to-door, especially getting hold of people who are at work right now. I want us to get back on them tonight."

Martha responded with an impatient sigh. "I still can't see why the killer is going after these people." She paused, pursing her lips. "For the life of me I can't see a connection." Her eyes widened. "Do you suppose this is all part of some elaborate scheme to mask the murder of one person, a sort of smokescreen to hide the truth? But then what about the cats? They're what got me on this in the first instance, but how do they fit in now?"

"Take a step back," suggested Tony. "You may be right when you say there's an elaborate plan in place. But most killers are rarely as bright as they think they are. As for the cats, who can say? Put them to one side, not quite out of sight but there when you need them. Like I said earlier, having a theory is always seductive, but you've made great progress by doing things the hard way. Keep going, it will all become clear."

Before she could respond, Krisha appeared. "Now things are calming down, can I get after camera footage and witnesses?" She didn't wait for an answer. "I thought I'd start on the other side of the road. From here I can see the house opposite has one of those stickers that says the place is protected by cameras connected to the cloud."

Martha squinted at the house Krisha was indicating.

"You've got the most amazing eyesight. I can't see a thing."

Krisha grinned at her. "Honestly," she said. "I can't see it either . . . but I noticed it earlier when I was working to get information about the hit-and-run case."

"Maybe you'll get the break we need. As someone once told me, the bad guys need to be lucky all the time, we only need to get lucky once."

Krisha looked puzzled.

"That may be the other way round," said Martha, who was starting to think it may not have been such good advice.

Finding herself briefly alone she wondered again about Tony Green. He was a bit prone to making statements of the obvious, and it was easier to see him as a 'by the book' cop rather than a criminal mastermind. But nothing in this case was quite how it first appeared. She wondered how Harry was getting on with his own investigation.

CHAPTER 26

Julie took the call on the second ring. "I take it this is business?"

"It is," said Martha. "There's been another killing. It's looking increasingly likely a young woman is behind all this. We've got witness accounts for this new killing and the hit-and-run.

"We've got a CCTV image, not that good unfortunately, but you need to be aware. I've forwarded the image — you'll see it's a bit ambiguous over whether we're looking for a man or a woman. In my opinion they're female, but I can't say for sure. Anyway, the short version: we have a witness who thinks they spotted a woman in a hoodie hanging around the scene of this latest killing. So, if you see anyone like this at the school or their home, hit the panic button."

"Not the best picture but good enough. No one like that around here at the moment, but if I spot someone . . ." Her voice trailed off — no need for further explanation. Julie was formidably tough, not a woman to be taken lightly.

"One more thing, and I hate saying this . . . but it feels like our friend may be back." An explosive shout from Julie almost made Martha pull the phone away from her ear. "Actually, I'm ninety-nine per cent convinced. So, I feel the same way, I can assure you. I spoke to Harry last night. The truth is, I've suspected this since I was assigned to the cats

– but I've held off saying anything. I've left it too long, if I'm honest."

"You didn't want it be true," said Julie. "No one wants that bastard in their life. Don't go beating yourself up."

"Thanks, Julie." Nailing the issue straight away, in her usual style. "I am guilty of all those things. Look, I've got Harry on the case, and we probably need to get the band back together."

"That's me, Harry, you and . . . Justin?" said Julie, who was firmly of the opinion that Martha should lose the 'ex' bit of her ex-husband, Justin. "We'll need Justin, not least for looking after Betty."

"Yes, Justin as well. You and Harry would never forgive me otherwise. I'll keep you in the loop, but we need to talk face to face as well. I'll sort it out. Anyway, better go."

With the call ended, Martha spent a few seconds watching the forensics team go about their painstaking work. She bowed to no one when it came to valuing their work but knew she would never have the patience for it herself. She spotted the now-familiar David Drinkwater quietly leading his team.

A raised eyebrow showed he'd seen her, and Martha turned away. They had a job to do and her hanging around would be a distraction. If she wanted fast results, she needed to leave them to it.

She had a thought and texted Julie: *If that person does turn up there, I want them in one piece, so I can talk to them.*

The response was fast: *No worries*, accompanied by a smiling emoji.

Martha looked at the message thoughtfully. She was glad she'd prepped Julie. If anyone could keep those two children safe, it was her friend.

With that thought out of the way she allowed herself to think about one of the issues that was really nagging at her: the speed with which these killings were taking place. She'd seen a headline in the online version of the *Daily Mail*. It said there was a 'crazed killer on the loose'. That word 'crazed' was sticking with her. What was really worrying was that far from being crazy, she was becoming ever surer that each murder was carefully planned and professional — the killer was on some sort of mission, but they were really enjoying their work. This latest, the beheading, was almost theatrical in its execution. It suggested things could only get worse.

She gave herself a mental kick up the backside. There was plenty to do in the here and now without worrying about the 'what ifs' of this case. She went to see how Mrs Henderson was coping.

She made her way into the neighbours' home and found the Smiths quietly doling out tea and biscuits. They couldn't do much apart from try to provide some calm. To her surprise Deidre Henderson was looking at her intently. She was a small, delicate-looking woman, but now she was showing her inner steel. The way she narrowed her eyes and tilted her head told the detective that this witness could handle a few gentle questions.

Martha made eye contact with Krisha and then looked at Mrs Henderson. The message was clear: *You talk to her*.

Krisha didn't hesitate. "I understand you've lived in your home for many years."

"That's right. Over forty years we've been here."

"And no trouble in that time? No threats of any kind?"

"Never had a problem. The only issue we ever had was my own fault. I left the front door open with my handbag on the floor, just inside the hall. Someone took it, but that was more than ten years ago."

"And no problems recently? Maybe a minor traffic accident? People can get very upset, more than they need to."

The bereaved wife shook her head, but before she could say any more the paramedic appeared.

"Sorry to interrupt," he said to Krisha, who waved away his concern. He turned his attention to Deidre.

"Do you want to go to hospital? Get them to check you over?"

"No, thank you. I'm OK physically and I want to help the police if I can."

"That's fine. But do call your GP. Tell him I've checked all your vital signs and you're in good shape."

The medic left Krisha to her questions.

"Your neighbour believes he may have seen a woman in this vicinity after your husband left this morning. Did you notice anyone hanging around? And am I right in thinking your husband went out for a cycle ride at the same time every day?"

Deirdre Henderson clenched her tiny fists. "Yes, he always headed out at the same time. I suppose you're having to consider if his punctuality was what killed him." She lost some of her defiance and her shoulders slumped.

"We have to consider all the options."

By way of answer Deidre shrugged and said quietly, "If there was someone, I didn't see them. Sorry."

Krisha felt like taking the woman in her arms, but she couldn't.

"Let's take a break for a minute. Catch your breath. If you don't mind, the family liaison officer will come and stay with you for a while, make sure you're OK, and we'll be there to talk to if anything springs to mind. I'm determined we'll get the person who did this to your husband."

CHAPTER 27

Imelda was so excited she felt like a well-shaken bottle of champagne that was ready to explode. She'd gulped down glass after glass of red wine in a bid to take the edge off, but she could barely feel its effects. Nothing could take the fizz out of becoming a serial killer.

Despite her pleasure she was mindful of the need to keep grounded: she didn't want anyone to think she was a high-maintenance operator. So far, the mystery man had proven to be her sort of boss. Even though they had only communicated over the phone, she could sense an underlying darkness to him, just waiting to be unleashed on the unwary.

What she wanted — to take the pressure off — was someone to share her feelings with, a role ideally suited to her mother, except that Audrey had gone into a sulk. Ever since Imelda had returned from decapitating the bike rider — she couldn't believe how much blood could come out of a body — Audrey had been tight-lipped, only occasionally interrupting her silence to issue a self-pitying rebuke.

"You don't need your old mum anymore. Me who went through agonies bringing you into this world."

It was never good when Mummy mentioned her birth. Audrey had struggled with a prolonged labour and often brought it up when she thought Imelda was overstepping the mark.

Audrey had been furious that she had spoken to the mystery man. "I'm not going to tell you who he is. *I'm* his friend. He confides in me, tells me his secrets. What does he want with a silly little girl like you? You're going to ruin everything with your selfish refusal to wait. What made you kill that man on the bike? It was too soon . . . you're bound to have made a mistake."

Imelda had bristled at this. The mystery man, this friend of her mother's, had already *told* her she'd done a brilliant job. She didn't need her mother undermining her out of jealousy. "Come on, Mummy, you know I always listen to you. It's just things were going a bit slowly; you were asleep. I talked to your friend, and he agreed. Chaos is what he wanted, and chaos is what I've given him. He said he was so pleased he was thinking about awarding us some sort of bonus. Imagine that."

But her mother had withdrawn into a sullen silence. Imelda knew she was going to have wait the moodiness out. When she put her mind to it Audrey could go at least twenty-four hours without a word. She seemed in the mood to do that here.

CHAPTER 28

"You two have got murders coming out of your ears. There's people who go their whole careers seeing fewer victims."

Tony Green was directing his remarks at Martha and Krisha as the trio sat in the mobile command unit in Dulwich Village. He looked between the two detectives. "This is a situation that would challenge anyone, so I thought we should go through each murder in isolation, and. it also helps me get up to speed." He blew on his Styrofoam cup of coffee, wincing slightly as he took a sip of the scalding drink.

Martha used the slight pause to gather her thoughts. Then she spoke from memory.

"We start with the Brown family. No killing, but unpleasant threats. It feels like a long time ago now, but a few days ago I told you I was involving a private security guard."

"From what I've heard anyone trying to get past your Julie probably has a death wish."

"There are very few men or women who would willingly take Julie on, that's for sure." Martha nodded in agreement before picking up the briefing. "We don't have any obvious suspect in that case. But thinking about it now, maybe we need to know more about Mr Brown, maybe he's got himself mixed up in something. Some of these guys play a bit close to the edge. Just because he has a nice house, nice family and loads of money, doesn't mean he can't be a criminal." She looked at Green. "Sorry to ask you, sir, but would you mind getting someone to dig into that? It'll have more authority coming from you."

"No problem," said Green. "I'll get straight on it after you talk us through where we are with the investigation."

Martha looked uncertain. "What I have probably doesn't warrant the word theory, at least not one based on hard evidence, it's more I don't want to lose sight of anything. What does puzzle me is why Brown only received threats and yet in the other three cases people have died. I keep coming back to how powerful he is. Brown is the richest victim by a country mile, which should make him the top target — at least, if you judge these things by money." She sighed.

"I guess I don't quite know what to think, except this one seems different, and it's not just because no one has died." She threw her hands in the air. "Are these other killings designed to keep him in line? During training we were told that if you could come up with a complicated theory that fitted all the evidence, it probably meant you were way off target. I don't know enough about him."

"I can help with that last bit when I talk to those financial experts. Thanks to the commissioner I hear we're getting access to the Met's leading forensic accountant, who can spot holes in spreadsheets from fifty paces. She has the skills and the experience to sniff out any suggestions of corruption."

"That would be fantastic," said Martha, sweeping her arm around the space. "So, case two, the murder of Maria Nightingale. At first it looked like she fell out of her window while under the influence of drugs and alcohol. She had ingested a huge amount of codeine from her drink being spiked. Also telling, and this is thanks to great work by Krisha, the bruising on her body suggests she was pushed out of the window, and we found shoe prints that indicate a second person was standing by the open window. The big question is: did this second person push Maria to her death?"

Martha waited a moment to see if anyone wanted to raise anything, but the team was happy for her to press on.

"Now, in terms of suspects, we obviously have to check out the husband and his alibi. He says he was with his girlfriend, but when DC Thomas and myself interviewed him, we came away with the impression he was hiding something. We need to find out what. He didn't help his case by suggesting the death of his wife opened up new possibilities for him. We need to stress-test that alibi since you can clearly see a scenario where he wants rid of a problem wife and finds a new shoulder to cry on. What does concern me is how aware he was of his wife's problems with drink and drugs. He even seemed to know that she was using private doctors to get her hands on drugs. We need to find these doctors and get your experts to dig into the financials."

"The way you lay it out makes him look like a 'person of interest' . . . if not the prime suspect," said Tony.

Martha looked thoughtful. "Right now he's ticking a lot of boxes. But I have serious reservations. I can't see him as a wife killer, and least of all a serial killer . . ." She held up her hand. "And don't worry, I will make sure he's innocent beyond doubt before I take him out of the firing line.

"What makes things awkward is there's definitely something the husband is hiding. He changed his story under questioning, only admitting he went to see his girlfriend when pushed. In other words, he lied. It's also possible that he had enough time to leave his meeting, get back to Dulwich to kill his wife and return to his meeting before he was missed. And remember he boasted about his money giving him access? Maybe he used some of his cash to pay a hitman?"

"I can see your dilemma here and quite right to stick on him for now," said Tony. "Any theories that might explain his behaviour?"

"I've thought of something else," said Martha. "Some of these financial firms have pretty strict rules about relationships with co-workers, especially if it's the boss getting friendly with a junior employee. Wasn't there a case recently where a top banker had to pay back millions in bonuses because he was caught out?"

She clapped her hands. "That may be the answer here. It certainly helps to explain why we're getting the sense that he's hiding something." She laughed. "We're back to the old adage, follow the money, at least when you're dealing with mega-wealthy City types."

Despite the laughter, the underlying mood was deeply serious. She pressed on. "So, we have our second murder, Geoffrey Renton, the victim of a deliberate hit-and-run. We have no links to the other two cases apart from it being in the same area and in the same time frame. We have a witness who has given us compelling evidence that the killer lay in wait for Mr Renton, who always took his dog for a short walk at the same time each evening."

Her face clouded. "I know it's not a lot to go on, but it's enough to at least keep us thinking. What I also need to say is that we don't know much about the victim. He led a quiet life with just his dog for company. No suggestion that he was involved in anything that got him killed.

"Now, let's talk about the gruesome killing of Colin Henderson, a successful civil engineer, now retired. There is an element of risk-taking to this one. The killing was enacted while Krisha was at the further end of the road, so our killer could have been caught. And we have more eyewitness testimony. What I am intrigued by is the notion that our killer is changing their approach."

Tony sat forward, his interest piqued, but giving Martha space to set her theory out before bombarding her with questions.

"First," said Martha, counting off on her fingers, "we have the fact that one murder follows another. Second, we have witness statements, and third, it feels different. Not as controlled as in the Brown family and Maria Nightingale. What strikes me about those first two cases is the careful planning. Now it feels like caution's being thrown to the wind."

Tony was jotting down some notes then looked up. "It's simply too much of a coincidence to have all this happening in such a small geographical area. And like you I'm wondering why no one has been killed in the Brown case. So, what do we need to do next?"

Martha had anticipated the question. "I want a hard focus on Stewart Nightingale — we need to either bag him or bin him. We need to talk to this girlfriend and find out what she knows, and I want a full work-up on any links he may have to our other victims. And we need to do it quickly."

CHAPTER 29

It was close to midnight by the time Martha got home. It had been a long day made frustrating by the fact that the volume of questions was not met by a similar quantity of answers. As she kicked her shoes off in the hallway, she tried to decide if she had the energy for a hot bath or just wanted to slump into bed fully clothed. The prospect of sleep was beguiling, but she sharply pushed the thought down. She was worried about her daughter Betty and needed to talk to Harry, who as always had stepped up to stop a problem escalating into a crisis. Once again, he had dropped everything to be there for Betty. She was fortunate that her daughter loved him.

Quite what would have happened without Harry she didn't like to think. Both she and Julie were locked into the murder investigation, and Justin was away in Las Vegas at some tech festival and wasn't due back for another couple of days. He'd offered to cut his trip short, but she wouldn't hear of it.

She'd spoken to her daughter on the phone earlier on and again at bedtime and she'd sounded fine, but Martha's maternal instincts were not going to let her off the hook too easily. It wasn't that long ago Betty had been kidnapped, and she'd been in the house when her grandmother was gunned down. That would have been a lot for an adult, let alone a child.

Harry was waiting in the kitchen and handed her a cup of hot, sweet tea.

"Drink that then get to bed. Betty's fine; she's loving all those FaceTime calls. Julie's promised her ice cream in the park next weekend. So, don't worry about us, everything's under control."

She slapped her head. "Hang on a minute, Harry, I've only gone and left a couple of files on the front seat. I need to go and get them."

Even as Harry's lips moved to say he would go, she was off, out of the front door and walking left towards Rosendale Road, where she'd found a parking spot three hundred meters down. A night bus barrelled past, but it seemed otherwise quiet.

She was approaching her car when a voice called her name. It belonged to a man sitting in the passenger seat of a dark-coloured panel van. "Martha, is that you? I'm so pleased to see you."

She looked down and saw a stranger, at which point her training with Harry kicked in: check your surroundings. She noted the driver's seat was empty, which meant the driver was out of the car.

It was obviously a trap, but Martha's subconscious was already calling the shots. It told her to find the driver. The passenger gave the game away when he couldn't stop himself looking at a spot immediately behind Martha's left shoulder.

That was threat number one. What about the second threat, the passenger? He was still sitting in the car, albeit reaching for the door handle. He obviously intended to get out and join the party, but he was about to find out that he had already left it too late. Martha's body was following instructions laid down by her brain.

Pivoting on her left foot she turned through almost 180 degrees to come face to face with a man holding a bag. He froze, and Martha seized the opportunity. She planted her left foot and launched her right upwards. A microsecond after he looked into her eyes, her foot slammed straight into his balls, with all the power and finesse of a professional foot-baller hitting a free kick.

She didn't wait to see the result. Spinning back to her starting position, she smashed her right foot hard into the passenger door, which was now halfway open. Behind her the driver was collapsing to the ground, his cheeks puffed out as the air was forced from his lungs. In front of her the previously smug passenger was screaming in agony. The edge of the door had trapped the fingers of his left hand, breaking three digits.

In less than five seconds, she had taken control, leaving the two hopeful kidnappers writhing in agony. The passenger's injury would see him out of action for weeks, and the driver would be peeing blood for days. She contemplated a few extra blows, but ruled it out.

She made a snap judgement. Instinct told her that this was the work of Neil Thompson, sending others to do his dirty work. She did not want her police colleagues involved, so leaving the badly battered duo behind, she went to her car and grabbed her files. She walked back past the would-be kidnappers and was pleased to see the driver retching into the gutter. Harry was going to be very pleased with her work. She continued her walk home, a little spring in her step.

CHAPTER 30

Harry produced one of his trademark evil grins as Martha recounted her one-sided battle with the pair of would-be kidnappers, inducing a wince as she described in vivid detail how she'd taken out the driver.

"Not that I'm too sympathetic, you'd have been entitled to kick him again . . . and again."

He listened carefully as she explained her decision to let the pair go.

"You were right to walk away. I'm sure that our friend Thompson is to blame, and you don't want your lot poking their noses into that yet. We might have a chance of getting to the bastard — if we play our cards right."

Martha, who was now full of adrenaline, raised an eyebrow.

"One of my best contacts got in touch about your Sergeant Edwards," said Harry. "He's definitely dodgy. My contact says he's been building up a nice little property empire, much bigger than he could have managed on a sergeant's pay. He's said to have six flats in a swanky new tower block close to East Croydon station . . . and that's just for starters."

Martha went back for the tea Harry had made her. It was still warm. "As you say, not bad for a humble sergeant."

"There's more," said Harry. "My contact used to work quite closely with your dad. He couldn't give me a lot but insists that sniffing around Edwards is dangerous. I pushed him on what he knew about our man's sudden disappearance, but he got very tight-lipped about that. All he'd say was that the sergeant was protected, so if they have punished him, he must be in trouble, maybe dead. Equally, they may have taken him out of the firing line. My contacts don't know or won't say."

Martha was reminded of how ruthless Thompson, this 'hidden enemy', could be.

"Do you think your conversation led to that little scene just now, when those goons tried to take me for a late-night drive?"

"It could be. Anyway, finish that tea before it gets too cold, and I'll check on our friends."

He was back a few minutes later and looking proud. "You're my best ever student, I'll give you that. Did they say anything?"

"No, but I think they must have had some sort of surveillance going on me and set up their little plan to snatch me on the spur of the moment. Me coming back was probably a surprise. I bet they were planning on waiting until morning."

"It'll be interesting to see if there's a reaction to tonight's failure. I wonder if our hapless pair actually report it in. If you can carry on sniffing around it would help. Maybe make it plain we're looking to talk, not get in a skirmish. I could really do without getting into a fight right now, so perhaps warn them they're at risk of blundering into a major murder investigation, one that the commissioner is taking a personal interest in."

"Why do you think they're bothering you?" asked Harry. "I mean, after the fiasco of getting you sent to prison, you'd think they'd leave it be. You haven't got anything on them, so why the ongoing interest?"

"I'm not sure," said Martha. "But the longer this goes on the more convinced I am that my dad left behind some big secret, one we haven't figured out, and that's what they're all worried about."

"Perhaps it makes them nervous to think about John Munro's little girl being a copper. You've got all the best bits of your dad, without the baggage," said Harry. "When he started, John Munro was a brilliant detective, even I was impressed. It was only later that things got a little complicated."

"Well, I can assure you I intend to keep it simple," said Martha. "I see villains, I arrest villains."

"That sounds remarkably like something your dad used to say. He'd tell me, 'Policing is easy, Harry. Just arrest the bad guys.'" Harry looked at her steadily. "You know better than most I'm not the biggest fan of the police, but you're going to need to be extra vigilant if they're not going to be helping you, especially with Julie and I both busy."

"I will be careful, Harry, don't worry," said Martha. "I know I let my guard down tonight, but I won't let that happen again. As to you, nothing makes me feel better than knowing you're looking after my daughter. She couldn't be in safer hands. And there may be news about Julie soon. We're beefing up protection around the Brown family; she may well be surplus to requirements."

CHAPTER 31

Martha had stepped out of the shower when the phone rang just after 5.30 a.m. It was Julie. Drying her hands and dabbing at her face with a towel she took the call.

"Hey, detective girl!" came an exuberant shout. No matter the time, it was rare to find her in less than a very good mood and always directly to the point. "You should see how much security is at the Browns' house. I may be out of a job after today."

"I'm afraid that's probably my fault," said Martha.

Her comment brought a burst of laughter from Julie. "It might be, but I forgive you. The Browns were knee-deep in armed protection officers last night; we were in danger of getting in each other's way. There was almost an arm wrestle over who was going to guard who."

The idea of Julie in a face-off with an elite squad of Met police brought a smile to her features. "I'm afraid that's definitely my fault. When we ran through everything that's going on, it felt like we were leaving the Brown family too exposed." She was pleased her friend couldn't see that her normally pale complexion was getting pinker. "I'm sorry, I'm making this sound all wrong — like you're somehow to blame. What I'm trying to say is that this was a botched operation at the start and it's important the police take full control, including security. The top brass has ordered an upscaling in the protection level. I'm sorry I didn't warn you, but we're running to catch up."

"I forgive you," said Julie. "Anyway, there was one especially cute officer who turned up last night. I may have to ask him out." She roared with laughter.

Martha waited patiently for her friend to stop laughing. "How is Mr Brown reacting to the changes?"

"That's a good question. I think he has mixed feelings, to be honest. Pleased that you lot are taking it so seriously, worried that it might all escalate. He also reckons his kids have got so used to having me around — and this is amazing — he's willing to pay a retainer in case he wants me back at some point in the future," said Julie. "His wife doesn't want the kids leaving the house at all and is talking about bringing tutors into the home, at least for the time being. But that would take me off the school run."

"What do you think is best — for you, that is?"

"I'm not sure what I'd be bringing to the party. My bet is that once the head finds out there are armed cops everywhere she'll say the children should stay away until it's safe. So, it feels like my need here is at an end."

Martha took in a deep breath, and Julie asked, "There's something else, isn't there?"

Martha rolled her eyes. "Are you adding psychic skills to your list?"

"I know you, Martha Munro, and you only breathe in like that when you're about to say something I won't like."

Martha screwed her eyes tight and quickly launched into an account of the bungled attempt to grab her off the street.

"I wish I'd been with you, although you obviously handled it pretty well. As serious as that sounds, I'm also guessing there's a bit more to this?"

"You *are* getting psychic. Well, I've been asking Harry to dig around on Thompson. Anyway, the short version is, he may have drawn attention to himself."

She made a sudden decision.

"As soon as you can get away, can you come and meet Harry here at my place? He can fill you in on all the details so far, but we both think it's time to start being uber-careful. I think it may be serendipity that you're coming available."

"Consider it done. I know you'll be worrying about Betty, but to get her they'll have to get through Harry and me first."

For Martha it felt like a great weight had been lifted, one she hadn't been aware of carrying around. She felt hot tears threatening and furiously dabbed at her eyes with the back of her hand.

"You have no idea what that means to me."

"Don't you go getting all soft. I'll go and see Harry and we'll make plans to keep everyone safe. You concentrate on catching the killer and we'll see you when you get home."

"If it's like yesterday I might not be back until the small hours," said Martha.

"No worries. Harry and I don't need a lot of sleep — just remind me not to play chess against him, especially for money. The sneaky old bugger convinced me he was rubbish. I should have known better."

CHAPTER 32

That night Martha got home early — just after 10 p.m. As she walked into the kitchen Harry was hitting the timer on the microwave. "Lasagne," he said over his shoulder. "I suppose you've been eating crisps all day."

Martha held her hands up in mock surrender. "In my defence I did eat different varieties — plain, salt and vinegar, cheese and onion . . ."

Julie was sitting at the table nursing a large mug of coffee which she set down with surprising finesse. "I can vouch for the lasagne. Anyway, Harry and I have been talking, and as you suggested, the timing of everything is turning out right. With all those cops at the Browns', the last thing they need is me getting in the way, so this gives me something to do."

Martha nodded along. "I have to admit I'm glad you're back on board. I'm sure the children will miss you, but they're getting very good protection so your talents can be deployed here. How are the Browns coping?"

"Mrs Brown is taking it pretty hard, I think," said Julie. "I don't see her much, but she's taken to waiting by the front door when we get back from school. Even with all the police around she grabs them in a bear hug the moment they walk through the door. Then she bursts into tears, which worries the kids. This afternoon, my last run, Mr Brown rushed out of his study and calmed things down, but he said to me his wife was feeling 'stretched' and he has the doctor coming. But the truth is, until this gets resolved, how is she supposed to cope?"

"I can guess what she's going through," said Martha. "When I was worried about Betty it was knowing you and Harry were there to look out for her that kept me together . . . That being said, I really need to talk to her. I need to show her a picture of someone we think might be the main suspect. I'd also like to see if she's aware of anything that might connect all the victims, and I include the Brown family in that."

Julie shook her head. "Not being funny, but you need to wait for this doctor to see her. She's devoted to those kids, and the thought of someone threatening them is overwhelming her. I don't want to be a drama queen about it, but I don't know how much more she can take."

"Of course," said Martha. "I guess I need to deploy a family liaison, someone she can talk to quietly."

"Don't go feeling guilty, you need to catch this killer — or killers — so I understand you can't afford to waste opportunities. What might help is if I prime the husband first, tell him you're hoping to talk to his wife but wanted to run it past him first. That way he gets the chance to say no if he doesn't think she's up to it."

"OK," said Martha. "That's a very good idea. If you call me as soon you know what the doctor has said. I'll speak to Mr Brown anyway, but I've got plenty to get on with in the meantime."

As she sat down Harry put a dark-coloured tea in front of her.

"That might be a bit too strong, so I'll have it if you don't want it."

Martha took a sip and handed it back. "No offence, Harry, but if I drink that there'll be no sleep till Christmas."

Harry studied his newly acquired tea with a speculative expression. "Julie and I will start thinking hard about the

Thompson situation. If needs must, do you mind if I act first then explain later?"

Martha didn't hesitate. "Do whatever you need to do. There is no one I trust more than you."

CHAPTER 33

Martha was getting used to the sensation of going to bed, her head hitting the pillow before being 'instantly' jerked awake by the alarm. Fifteen minutes after the buzzer sounded, she was on her way. All thoughts of Neil Thompson were soon driven to the back of her mind as she teamed up with Krisha to manage the workload for the day ahead.

They were using the mobile incident room in the village.

"The autopsy for Maria Nightingale gets underway in an hour, plus we should get the full results of her blood tests," said Krisha.

Martha pulled a face as she put down the sticky bun she'd taken a bite out of. "That's sweet and stale. No wonder so many coppers end up being warned about diabetes. I don't suppose we have anything else to eat?"

Krisha cleared her throat, making Martha look up.

"You're right. Mind on the job. Now, autopsy . . . Tony texted earlier, and he's fine about attending the autopsy, which leaves us free to keep pushing the investigation, and boy does it need a push." She looked down at her notebook. "Are we still on course to interview Stewart Nightingale?"

Krisha automatically glanced at her own notes even though she had the answers ready. "We're seeing Mr Nightingale at

Walworth Road at noon today. I had thought he would try and delay things, but he's made himself available. His girlfriend is a Valerie Johnson. I sent her a text last night and will follow up if I don't hear back by 10 a.m."

"Good, that's very good," said Martha. "We should certainly speak to Nightingale first, then we have something to check against. I presume he's bringing a lawyer."

A quick nod from Krisha confirmed she was right.

"I never like to overprepare these things, but we need some details out of him, like how long had the affair been going on? Where did they meet for their trysts? And was he planning on leaving his wife, or at least had he told his girlfriend he was? He also told us his wife got worse after injuring her knee and started getting prescriptions from private doctors. I want to know a lot more about that. His description of how his wife plunged into addiction sounded a bit glib to me. But maybe he's just privately upset about what happened to her.

"Anyway, how shall we play it in the interview? I'm wondering if you take the lead and I'll observe. He'll be expecting a 'good cop/bad cop' routine, so the longer I can stay aloof the more pressure he's going to feel . . . I hope. Above all, let's get this done. Every instinct is telling me he's not our killer. Just another middle-aged bloke who's cheating on his wife. What about the girlfriend? What does she do?"

Krisha pulled a face. "She works for a hedge fund that shorts other companies. That's the technical bit. I googled it and it still didn't make a lot of sense, except that it sounds like a form of gambling. If you guess right and a company's share price collapses, you make a big profit. There's stuff about borrowing shares, but I lost the will to live after that."

"I can only imagine the pillow talk between those two," said Martha. "By the way, the chief inspector wants an update with a view to the deputy chief constable making some sort of statement. What do you think we can give him?"

"We'll have the autopsy results soon," said Krisha. "Plus, we can add something about pursuing multiple lines of inquiry?"

"That sounds more like we haven't got a clue," said Martha.

"I take your point. The media team always go on about the way you use words. Perhaps we talk about taking key witness statements today, going door to door, and of course we have the picture. We can say we're very confident it's an excellent likeness and advise the public to keep well clear. Hopefully someone recognises who it is so we can go and grab them."

"That's great. I can live with that. It sums up where we are without giving away anything sensitive," said Martha. "Anything else we should brief the chief inspector about?"

"With a bit of luck, we'll pick up something on CCTV today," said Krisha. "I've been pushing hard on that."

CHAPTER 34

Imelda woke up, stretched and sniffed her armpits. The stink of body odour made her gag — she needed a shower.

She'd got home just after 10 a.m. and collapsed into her chair as she experienced a sudden comedown after running on an adrenaline high. It was midday so she'd been asleep for two hours. She turned to look at her mother, who was studying her with watery eyes.

"You smell worse than you look, girl, and you look pretty bad. If you want to play the part of the killer for hire you need to look the part. Go and get yourself tidied up, then we can talk. You've been so wrapped up in your work that you ain't thinking straight. You've done the work before getting paid, so we really need to think about that."

"You don't look so good yourself!" Imelda snapped. The barb about not getting paid had struck home. Before she could say anything else, Audrey had fixed her with the type of laser-focused glare only a mother could manage. She left the conversation until later and headed for the shower.

Half an hour later, considerably more fragrant and dressed in clean clothes, Imelda's stomach was growling for food.

"Fancy fish and chips, Mum?" she called out, only to be staggered when her mother declined.

"I've lost my appetite recently. Don't worry about me. I might have a sherry or two. Check how much I've got. I might need a top-up."

"No worries," said Imelda, stepping out. She thought the way her mother had been drinking recently she'd better pick up half a dozen bottles from the discount store near the market. That should keep her going for two days — hopefully.

Back home with her food, Imelda switched on the lunchtime news. Audrey still hadn't grasped the idea of being able to access the news at any time anywhere, so long as you had Wi-Fi. Instead, she was a creature of rigid habits, and if she was at home during the day, then it was the BBC headlines at 1 p.m. Imelda switched channels and caught the tail end of yet another programme about antiques. It quickly segued into the lunchtime bulletin. Imelda started choking on a chip. There she was on TV news — Scotland Yard's most wanted.

"You stupid, stupid girl," said Audrey. "You see what happens when you get ideas above your station? I told you not to move so fast."

Imelda felt like she was encased in concrete; she couldn't move at all. What was she going to do? She really needed to talk to the mystery man. Surely it was time he revealed himself?

CHAPTER 35

Martha missed the news alert since she was in an interview room with Krisha, Stewart Nightingale and his lawyer, Tony Wilkinson, an uncommunicative man dressed in a dark business suit. She folded her arms and her eyes narrowed slightly as she listened to Nightingale respond to the opening salvo of questions. As they had agreed, Krisha was taking the lead while Martha silently looked on. Nightingale had arrived late and apologetic. After being shown to the interview room, Nightingale had made a great point of removing his jacket to hang on the back of his chair.

Marth suspected he was trying to disguise his anxiety.

Krisha had begun with a series of looseners about Nightingale's job and the nature of the bank he was in charge of.

Martha listened to the bland responses about a talent-spotting initiative in deprived areas, then decided now would be a good time to make her first intervention. "Very interesting that you mention doors," she said. "It must be marvellous for some of these young people to find themselves being shown into your world." She paused and tugged at her ear. "I can't help wondering if the experience worked both ways. It's not every day that a leading banker gets to meet the people at the bottom of the pyramid, as it were."

Nightingale shrugged off her question, and Martha could sense this line of inquiry was getting nowhere. She couldn't get past the firm belief that this man was no killer. It was making her impatient to get back on the investigation and find the real murderer.

Just as things seemed to be winding down, Krisha lobbed in an apparently routine question.

"Could you tell me about your girlfriend, Valerie Johnson?"

Nightingale was stony faced. Martha understood that he knew what was coming. He wanted them to make the move. Martha casually folded her hands on the table as she nodded at Krisha, who asked, "I was wondering about the monthly payments you've been making to Ms Johnson. We estimate you've been giving her £100,000 a time. Could you explain that to me?"

Nightingale held up his hand.

"You've been very thorough, I see. The truth is I intended to leave my wife. She'd become a drunken liability and was getting worse. But it wasn't just me who needed to get out, it was my children as well. It was no longer safe for her to look after them.

"Valerie, to her immense credit, was willing to help me and the boys escape. She found us a penthouse flat near Tower Bridge and I sent her the money to pay for the deposit and the mortgage."

"Why all the secretiveness?" said Martha. "Why not tell her you were leaving and have done with it?"

"I hate to say this," said Nightingale, "but she was no longer the woman I married. The drugs and drink had created mental health problems. Several times she threatened to kill herself if I ever left her. I wasn't sure she meant it, but what else could I do? I couldn't take a risk, not with the boys."

"So, this penthouse — is it in your name, or your girl-friend's?" Martha asked.

"It was in Valerie's name, and before you jump to con-clusions, there was a good reason for that," said Nightingale. "My wife may have driven herself mad, but she was formida-bly determined and clever. How else do you think she got her hands on so many drugs? The point is this: the moment she knew I was leaving she'd brief her lawyers and they'd freeze my assets. Having this in Valerie's name was the safest way of keeping it out of my wife's hands."

Martha quickly drew the interview to a close. She and Krisha had to talk.

"What did you make of that, then?" asked Krisha.

Martha threw her hands in the air. "Honestly, I'm even more convinced about his innocence. It's frustrating that we still can't entirely rule him out, but I have the strongest feel-ing we won't have long to wait."

Her phone beeped. She checked the sender then raised her eyebrows. "It's from him. We're a lot closer than I'd realised." Martha angled the phone screen towards Krisha.

"What the hell!" Krisha exclaimed.

"You took the words out of my mouth." Martha re-read the message and read it out loud. "*I've been misleading you. I need to come back and set the record straight.*"

"Are you thinking what I'm thinking?" asked Martha.

"I think it sounds mightily close to a confession, just not sure what exactly he's confessing to."

"He's a conundrum that needs solving quickly, that's for sure," responded Martha as her busy fingers sent a reply: *Where are you?*

The response was instant. *I'm outside in my car. My lawyer's gone.*

"Let's get him in now," said Martha. "We either arrest him or eliminate him altogether."

Ten minutes later and Nightingale was back in the inter-view room facing the two detectives. Nightingale produced a tissue and fastidiously — irritatingly, thought Martha

— wiped his fingers. Satisfied, he stared intently at the pair and announced, "I'm guilty."

Martha's heart beat faster. Krisha had clenched her fists. They said nothing, both sensing Nightingale wasn't done. Not yet. The silence seemed to stretch out, but in reality lasted seconds, then he spoke again.

"Like I said, I am guilty, though probably not guilty of what you may be thinking. That interview now made me realise I had to level with you guys or I'm wasting everyone's time."

Martha let go of the breath she'd been holding in and checked the recording device to make sure the light was on, as she'd known it would be.

"You need to explain that, sir. I don't want any confusion, and right now I'm confused."

"Sorry, I'm not doing it deliberately," said the banker.

Martha kept her expression as neutral as she could manage, encouraging him to carry on. For the first time he looked vulnerable and had lost his air of shiftiness. Either he was a good actor, or they were finally getting a glimpse of the real man.

Nightingale puffed his cheeks and then launched into his story — hesitantly at first, then slowly gaining in confidence. "My relationship with my girlfriend and my wife, well . . . it's complicated," he said looking down, so he missed both women rolling their eyes. "I expect you've heard it a thousand times, but it is — or was, I suppose I should say.

"When I first met Valerie, we had a strictly business relationship. Valerie provided me with insights, rumour and reliable information that was very helpful to me. It allowed me to make solid investments and take opportunities I might otherwise have ignored."

"This information. I assume it was gleaned from her own work at the hedge fund? I'm not an expert on financial law, but that sounds perilously close to breach of contract, maybe even insider trading," said Martha.

"That's not quite the case," said Nightingale. "Valerie isn't an employee and most of the information is out there, you just need to know where to look and how to look. You'd be amazed how many financial scandals could have been avoided if investors had paid proper attention to the warning signals. Valerie is a bit of a genius at that.

"But yes, you're right. It is a grey area and that's why I wasn't honest with you when we first spoke. The last thing I wanted to do was draw attention to our relationship. Once we became romantically entangled it caused more problems. Shareholders hate the thought of pillow talk . . . that CEOs might risk giving away secrets. I'm sure I could have defended our actions, but I'd rather not go there at all.

"That's why I was evasive to start with. I mean, we both might have lost our jobs and faced a financial miscon-duct investigation, at the very least. You can see why I was worried."

He glanced between the two detectives then carried on. "When you hit me with the money I'm paying to Valerie, I was stunned. I hadn't expected you to find that quite so fast, if at all. I knew as soon as you mentioned it the game was up, but I couldn't bring myself to tell you."

"Yet you changed your mind. Care to explain that?" asked Martha.

"Simple really. I realised I sounded like a husband with reason to murder his wife and leave himself free to marry his mistress. Once I thought that—" he threw his hands in the air — "there was no reason to keep things quiet anymore. I owed you a proper explanation and an apology."

He stopped talking and Martha was happy to let the silence grow. She had one key question.

"You say you're keen to set the record straight. But you're right, I do wonder if you had the motivation to murder your wife. And nothing you've told me changes that. In fact, it makes it seem more likely, given that you've introduced this transactional element into the relationship between you and your girlfriend. So, my question is this: what reason can you come up with that says you didn't have the motivation to murder your wife?"

"Because she was dying anyway. According to her specialist, the damage done by her ever-growing dependence on drink and drugs meant it was nearly over for her. And believe me, I tried to stop her. I got rid of her stashes of booze and pills. But for each one I found, she had another.

"And I told you she was clever — well, for a junkie and an alcoholic. She planned ahead. She had so many supplies it didn't even make a difference when I cut her off — I told her private doctors what she was up to and threatened to report them to the regulator. All Maria did was dip into her reserves. I even tried reasoning with her . . . that was a waste of breath. She laughed at me while washing codeine down with vodka."

"You say the doctor told you she was killing herself. Which doctor, and how long had she got?" said Martha.

"It was after she took a blood test about six months ago which showed extensive liver damage and also revealed how much she was taking. The view was that unless she stopped, she had a maximum of eighteen months left. Maybe less than that. I did try to reason with her again, but she really didn't care. She wasn't the woman I married nearly twenty years ago.

"You might think I should have done more, but it was over. I knew it in my heart. If you've ever been near an addict, you know how bad it gets. They don't care so long as they get their next fix.

"So, the reason I didn't kill my wife? She was already doing a very good job of it herself. And I'm sure you're both wondering why I didn't just tell you up front." He stopped and sighed, his shoulders slumped. "You have to bear in mind that I was trying to keep this from everyone — the boys, her mum, her few remaining friends. That secrecy became a habit, one I couldn't stop. It wasn't that I found her embarrassing. It was way beyond that. All I could give her was a little dignity. Nothing more, nothing less."

CHAPTER 36

"Don't go disappearing, especially not abroad. That will make me very nervous." Martha sounded uncompromising but privately was thinking the husband had just avoided a murder charge. Nightingale was given strict instructions about staying close as the second interview drew to a close.

"We can, and will be, checking your story out. And as you know, your wife's autopsy will show the extent, if any, of her liver damage."

He nodded. "I have letters I can show you from various tests she had, and I will provide you with whatever help you need to talk to her doctors."

Martha stepped out to put in a quick call to her chief inspector to explain this latest turn of events and find out if the autopsy had revealed anything that supported his story.

"On the face of it, yes," said the chief inspector. "The doc said there was major liver damage, which was hardly a surprise given that we knew what she was doing to her body. He was going to do more tests, but you could tell he thought it was serious. He said the liver has tremendous powers of recovery, but you have to stop abusing it. Don't stop and things go south pretty fast."

He went on. "You guys have done well to get to the heart of this so fast. I was thinking he was a good fit for the murder, so it's important to get him out of the way. What's your impression of him now he's opened up?"

"Krisha and I were talking about that," said Martha. "We both think he's telling the truth now, or at least a version of it. He was open in the second interview and his version of events was quite plausible; he could have lost his job. As to him saying secrecy had become a habit, well, you should have met my dad. He didn't even like giving someone the time of day!"

This produced a short guffaw of laughter. "Sounds like my dad. Sometimes I can still see him telling me not to speak to anyone."

"Oh yes, that brings back memories for me," said Martha. "Krisha and I are glad to get him out of the way so fast. The first time we dealt with him? If I'm honest—" she bit her lip — "I thought he was guilty. A perfect example of why you never accept the first answer, not until everything else is done. Meanwhile, we've spoken to his girlfriend, and she's volunteered to come straight in."

"Excellent," said Tony. He promised to pass the information up the line.

After he ended the call, Martha felt a burning sensation in her gut. She realised it was midday and she'd eaten nothing except a tiny bite of that disgusting sticky bun. She just had time to make it to the nearby Subway — not her number one choice but it would do. Krisha joined her.

"To be honest I need to get out of the station for a minute. I get stir crazy when I spend too long inside," she told Martha.

Minutes later, they'd barely started eating when Martha got a call from the duty sergeant, Peter Rose.

"What is it?" asked Krisha.

"They have an ID for the killer."

CHAPTER 37

"We've had more than twenty responses and the same name is coming up: Imelda Taylor, and one caller said she lives near Tulse Hill overground station . . .' Even over the phone, Martha could sense his excitement to be delivering what could well turn out to be the key to catching the killer. "I've texted the chief inspector so he knows what's going on and he'll be ringing back in five minutes. He's in a meeting with the chief constable. They know what it's about."

"Good," said Martha. "Can you put a SWAT team on standby? Chief Inspector Green can authorise it. And don't send uniformed officers to the area until we have a proper plan in place. This woman is highly dangerous and should not be approached."

"Will do, ma'am. I'll make sure the message gets out — no heroics."

Martha ended the call and brought Krisha up to speed.

"It's so tempting to get an address and race up there," said Krisha. "Your theory about it being a woman looks to have paid off. We need to get her off the street as quick as we can, she's clearly extremely dangerous and out of control."

"It was a gut feeling — but I'd rather be proved right," said Martha. "I don't know about you but my heart's pounding ten to the dozen. We might be on the brink of resolving this. Come on, let's get over to the incident room. I want to be there when they find this Imelda."

Martha and Krisha walked into the incident room to find Sergeant Peter Rose standing with his hands on his hips and a frustrated scowl on his face. His expression didn't change as he caught sight of the two detectives. They hurried towards him.

"I take it there's a problem," said Martha.

"There is. We had a full address for her in Tulse Hill from five years ago. It was a council property, and she was sharing it with an Audrey Taylor, maybe her mother. After that — nothing. There is no further trace of them beyond the information that they moved out five years ago to parts unknown."

Martha felt an overwhelming sense of disappointment, which she covered by helping herself to a drink of water. By the time she had drained her cup her sense of optimism was restored. She should have known it wasn't going to be that easy, but there was still plenty to do.

"Can we move anyone who's available to the area? We need to give the new tenants a knock, and we should speak to the neighbours." She thought for a moment. "Make finding the school she went to a top priority. If they don't know what happened to her, they may know someone who does. If we're lucky they'll have a reasonably up-to-date photo of her. We always knew this was going to take good old-fashioned police work — let's get out there and use up some shoe leather. She's almost in our grasp, I can feel it!"

CHAPTER 38

In the space of twenty-four hours Martha had gone from the euphoria of thinking she was about to crack the case to despair as early breakthroughs turned into dead ends. Despite the technology at their fingertips, all they had established was that Imelda had been living with her mother at the Tulse Hill address. Since then, nothing. It felt like they had vanished into thin air.

They'd tracked down her old school pretty quickly, but even there the trail had run cold. Imelda had left the moment she turned sixteen and they had no knowledge of where she had gone. The head had made no pretence that she was sad to see her go, telling the police that Imelda was a vicious bully who escaped detection because the other kids were so frightened of her.

"She was quite capable of extreme violence, and after the first victim was taken to hospital with multiple fractures, everyone else fell into line. A couple of years ago one of the braver children told me Imelda's weapon of choice was a lump hammer."

The officer visiting the school had expressed amazement that the police weren't involved, even after the event, but the head had shrugged. "The school governors wanted it kept quiet. She was long gone by then, and stirring up old news would help no one."

On learning this detail, Martha had needed to be stopped from heading straight to the school and arresting the head and the governors.

"What will you arrest them for?" asked Krisha.

"I don't know, obstructing justice maybe, or being too cynical to run a school — that has to be an offence. How can they put keeping bad news out of the papers above children being harmed?" She clenched her fists so tight she dug her nails painfully into her palm.

Krisha gave her a knowing look. She understood that the outburst was down to frustration at the inquiry slamming to a halt. She tugged her earlobe. "We can always come back to them later. At the moment that feels like a secondary target. What do you think?"

"I think you're right." Martha slowly unclenched her fists and flexed her fingers. She was hunched over and defeated but sat up as a thought hit her. "We need to approach this differently," she announced, locking her gaze on Krisha, who gave an enthusiastic if confused nod.

Martha's enthusiasm was growing, like a flat tyre being reinflated.

"Don't you see?" said Martha, still gazing at the baffled Krisha. "Someone has gone to a great deal of trouble to hide any trace of these two. It's like something out of a spy story."

"You're totally right," said Krisha, who had experienced her own lightbulb moment. "There is some interesting stuff in the head's statement. She said the school photos of Imelda had vanished from their computer system, which has slowed down our searches. And maybe that's the point, to throw a little confusion around."

"At least the head has ID'd Imelda from our picture," said Martha. "Let's get the Met's media team to throw everything they can at Imelda being a 'most wanted'."

"We should definitely do that," said Krisha. "But what if Imelda is covering her tracks?"

"That's just it," said Martha, her expression steely. "What little we know suggests Imelda is more about muscle than brain. I have no problem thinking of her as a savage killer, but not so much as the brains of the operation."

"Ah," said Krisha, experiencing a second lightbulb moment. "You think someone else is involved."

CHAPTER 39

The second media push produced a deluge of tip-offs, with most quickly dismissed as being of the little green men variety, but three calls, all anonymous, were put on the A list.

"According to these three callers they often see her around Brixton market. The question is, what do we do about it? If we go in heavy-handed, she'll take to the hills," said Martha.

She looked down. "There's only one thing for it — go undercover. We can have plain-clothes officers in and around the area with armed officers waiting nearby as backup."

It was a simple plan, but it had one flaw — Health and Safety intervened and insisted on carrying out a thorough review. Tony rang Martha to explain.

"We've tried everything possible, even a direct intervention by the top brass, and nothing will move Health and Safety. We have no choice but to wait. You can have the area under observation but from a distance, and no direct action."

In the event, Martha was saved from a bout of rage when a new caller rang the tip-off line. He provided an address for Imelda and her mother.

"It's right by the market, a two-bedroom flat above an off-license. It's privately owned but the details disappear in a web of offshore companies," said Sergeant Rose.

"So, the mystery of who is helping Imelda deepens," said Martha. She puffed her cheeks in frustration. "I know we've been ordered to hold our horses, but let's get the flat under surveillance. Right now, we need Imelda, and from that point of view, I don't care whose flat she's living in."

With the commissioner's office keeping the pressure up, Health and Safety started to agree a plan within the hour. With surveillance in place, an extraction team was briefed. The plan was simple — smash the door open, storm the flat, subdue the occupants. The strike team were in full protective gear, armed with tasers and supported by specialist firearms officers.

Martha argued passionately that enough time had been wasted and urged immediate action. She won the day and the strike team moved in. Plans showed the front door opened directly to the living room with a small kitchen area to the rear. Behind that were two bedrooms with a shared bathroom.

Martha and Krisha waited in a van nearby as the specialist team set up. The silence was broken by the team leader.

"We're close to the front door and from here there's a powerful smell of decomposition coming from the flat. I'm quite sure there's a dead body in there."

Five minutes later, the flat was breached and Martha and Krisha were inside.

The first thing they saw was the decomposed body of an overweight woman, slumped in an armchair in front of the TV. Eerily, her face was locked in a grimace, suggesting she had been in terrible pain before her death. Martha gagged at the choking stink and was grateful for the mint that Krisha pressed into her hand. It didn't get rid of the cloying smell, but it made it tolerable.

A fast check of the tiny space had confirmed the dead woman was the only occupant. Martha watched the team leader approach. Even with his features obscured by a mask, she could see he was attempting to breathe through his mouth rather than his nose.

He gestured at the body. "She's been there for several days, for sure. We have indications that someone else was living here at the same time. There's food in the fridge which is well within date. More telling, there's a bottle of milk on the side which is still fridge-cold to the touch. It looks like we may have missed the primary target by a few hours."

Before Martha could respond, the strike leader gestured again at the body. "Someone's been leaving food for the dead woman. There's a bag of fresh pastries resting on her lap."

Martha swallowed hard. "So, not only do you think someone was living here with the dead body, they were giving it food as well?"

Hearing a sound, she looked to her right to see Krisha make a rush for the front door and some fresh air. She followed her out.

"Do you need five minutes?" Martha asked.

Krisha shook her head. "I needed to get out of there. I'm alright now."

Martha looked at her carefully. "You have lost that green tinge. Anyway, it seems obvious that the dead woman is Imelda's mother, Audrey, which makes Imelda herself the most likely person to have been living with her dead mother. Which probably makes Imelda deeply disturbed."

Krisha, now breathing through a face mask in a futile attempt to cut out the smell, shuddered. "Wasn't there a film where the son kept his dead mother around for advice?"

"*Psycho*," said Martha. The two shared a quiet moment until they were approached by the senior SOCO, who introduced herself as Anne Winters. "The smell is bad enough, but that look on her face. I'm not sure I'll be forgetting that in a hurry," said Martha. "Do you have any thoughts on cause of death?"

The SOCO reached into a pocket and produced a small, green pot. "Menthol?" she said with a gesture that took in Martha and Krisha. Both detectives accepted and discovered that daubing the gel under their nostrils partially protected them from the smell.

"Let me take another look — I always like to double-check my work. Come with me if you're up to it — or stay outside if you're worried about seeing breakfast again."

The two officers followed her in and did their best to pretend there wasn't a stomach-churning stench in the room as Anne took a long moment staring at the body, her lips moving as she talked inaudibly to herself. Then, apparently happy with her visual examination, she looked at Martha.

"You've noted her expression. That strongly suggests she had a seizure. Also note the patches of dark red skin showing through the decomp. Those two things alone suggest poisoning — by cyanide. We'll get her tested back at the lab."

"I appreciate you going out on a limb about this. We won't make it official until you say so, but it really helps." Martha paused. "Can you say how long she's been dead?"

"You probably noticed the bloody foam coming out of her mouth? Just here." Anne pointed at Audrey's face.

Martha, who had now seen it, was trying very hard to unsee it. Next to her, Krisha gulped.

"In general terms, that kind of leakage happens on day three and may go on for another couple of days. I'd make a guess, and this is only a guess, that given the foam and the general state of the body, this woman died about five days ago."

"So, our suspect may have killed her own mother and been living with her for all that time, buying her food as though there was nothing wrong," said Martha, unable to suppress a shudder.

"That's so yucky," said Krisha.

"And I'm feeling even more confident that this isn't a series of lone wolf attacks," said Martha. "From what we're picking up here, someone is manipulating Imelda. I know she's a killer, but I suspect she's being taken advantage of."

Even as she spoke the spectre of Neil Thompson seemed to loom ever larger. It was increasingly obvious that Thompson was like a puppeteer, pulling Imelda's strings. She wished she could share her fears with Krisha, but she needed Harry to dig up more information if she was going to consider the prospect of dragging someone else into her family history.

Anne walked up. "I know it's the highest priority. I'll see this through personally."

Martha's phone rang. She answered and listened intently, asked the caller to repeat themselves and ended the call with a decisive instruction. "Make Southwark Cathedral the rendezvous point."

The call had filled Martha with fresh energy.

"Am I right in thinking we may have our woman?" Krisha already sensed the answer.

"We've had a ring-in," said Martha, a broad smile on her face. "Informant says Imelda's holed up in one of those fancy pads near Tower Bridge." Seeing Krisha arch an eyebrow, she continued, "Our caller was a man who called himself Ted, for what it's worth. But more importantly, he knew key details. He knew it was Imelda and gave her name. He knew where she'd been living with her mum and — this is the weird bit — emailed over some footage of Imelda making a full and frank confession. It's being sent over now."

Before Krisha could say anything, both detectives' mobiles pinged to announce an email had arrived. Martha was fastest to bring it up and she and Krisha stood side by side as they watched the digital confession, uploaded to TikTok, no less.

Imelda was staring straight at the camera. "It was me. I killed those people because I wanted to. I expect you'll have lots of questions, but you'll have to come and get me first, so get a move on. I don't have all day." The clip ended abruptly.

Martha stared at the blank screen, astonished by the turn of events. She replayed the video and winced at the way Imelda seemed to luxuriate in her wickedness.

"I've never seen anything like that. That woman has so many loose screws I wouldn't be surprised if she rattled when she walked," said Krisha. "But then, if you're going to confess to being a serial killer, why not do it on social media?"

Martha had wrapped her arms around herself. "It was like she didn't have a care in the world. You'd think she was describing her weekly shopping list, not admitting to multiple murders."

Krisha was about to reply but stopped and looked at Martha intently, as if she'd figured out that her boss knew rather more than she was letting on.

CHAPTER 40

"She's sitting in the lotus position right in front of the living-room window. She hasn't moved for the last ten minutes. It's like she doesn't have a care in the world."

The SWAT team leader carried herself in a precise way that spoke of military training, her voice and observations giving nothing away. "Take a look for yourselves," said Sergeant Celia Newby, handing a pair of small but powerful binoculars to Martha, who trained them on a window on the second floor of the building close to Tower Bridge on the south side of the River Thames. She and Krisha were in a building on the opposite side of the river that afforded unhindered views of the flat Imelda was holed up in.

Martha couldn't help shuddering as she looked. "It's as though she's waiting for us," she said, passing the binoculars to Krisha. "What do you think, Celia, is it safe for your team to go in?"

"It's looking that way," said Newby, her eyes crinkling. "She doesn't appear to be wired up to anything, but I'd like to keep watching for a little longer — just to be sure. None of my team has ever seen anything like this, at least not in real life. It's the sort of thing you get in one of those old-school

Kung Fu movies — the 'noble' hero preparing to sacrifice himself in the fight against oppression."

"I think I know the sort of thing you're talking about, the chance to go down in glory with all guns blazing," said Martha. "Is that going to be an issue for you?"

"Only if we don't prepare for it," said the sergeant. "Once I'm happy she's not connected to a bomb we can go in. If she tries throwing a few moves, we zap her with a couple of tasers. That'll take the fight out of her. There's no way I'm allowing this scumbag to commit suicide by cop."

The harshness of her final words reminded Martha that underneath the uniform beat the heart of a human being.

As always, it was the waiting that got to you. Martha and Krisha kept checking the time on their phones as the minutes crawled by. It was time for the SWAT team to head in. They were well drilled and through the front door like it was made out of butter. Seconds later Imelda had her hands securely cuffed behind her back and Martha was reading Imelda her rights.

Imelda said nothing, continuing to stare at something that only she could see. Martha repeated the words only to get the same result. Total silence, with one difference — the second time around, a smirk had appeared. It was an especially annoying smirk. And it worried Martha for one reason. It was a smirk that said, *You're missing something, something very important.*

* * *

Krisha stood with Martha as they watched Imelda being led away, still smirking in that brainless manner.

Martha leaned against a wall and blew a sigh of relief. "I can't believe how quickly that woman has got under my skin. They're taking her to Brixton nick so it will take a while to get her booked in. What did you make of that smirk?"

"I found it disturbing, if I'm honest," said Krisha. "To kill three people then act like it's some sort of game, or something to be proud of. We need to make sure we keep that woman off the streets for the rest of her life."

"I certainly agree with all that . . ." said Martha.

"But . . . ?" said Krisha, sensing Martha was about to say more. She wondered if it was connected to that expression she'd seen on her face a short while ago.

"Did you get the feeling that Imelda was all there? Did you feel she might have been got at in some way?"

Krisha took her time answering. She wasn't quite sure where Martha was going with this, but she was certain this was part of another, as yet unseen, agenda.

"Are you suggesting some sort of mind control?" she said tentatively.

Martha's eyes, which had been locked on to Krisha, lost some of their sparkle.

"When you say it out loud it does seem a bit sci-fi. But I did go on a training course that talked about how it can be much easier than you might imagine to manipulate people. Sometimes it's as simple as spiking a cup of tea with a drug that lowers inhibitions. Or maybe it's a form of brainwashing. The instructor made the point that people who have the capacity to kill may be quite disturbed and vulnerable to mental control."

She stopped talking and screwed her eyes shut for a moment.

"I need to leave that sort of diagnosis to the experts . . . but you have to admit that Imelda gives off a very strange vibe. I've encountered killers before and none seemed so detached from reality, almost as though she's not part of the real world and exists in her own space . . . that's what got me thinking about the course."

A fleeting smile passed over Martha's face.

"Thanks for bearing with my flight of fancy there. Let's get over to Brixton via a stop-off for some strong coffee. I think we've got a long day ahead of us."

Although she was all smiles, Krisha was more convinced than ever that Martha was keeping something back, something related to that incident where she'd ended up in prison after her mum was killed.

The Met was rife with rumours about that, some so outlandish Krisha dismissed them out of hand, especially the one that had Martha fronting a drug-smuggling operation set up by her father.

She had always been more convinced by the suggestion that Martha's father — who Krisha regarded as being close to a hero for the way he'd stood against police corruption — was a man who had attracted enemies the way others collected stamps.

But, she thought, what possible connection could there be between Martha and a serial killer in Dulwich? If there *was* a connection, why wasn't Martha taking steps to protect herself and her family? Maybe her colleagues were in the firing line? OK, the latter was a bit daft, but she did need to keep her wits about her.

As usual she had too many questions and too few answers. She was close to coming out with it and asking — and she wouldn't take no for an answer.

CHAPTER 41

As they approached Brixton police station in the normal heavy traffic flow, Martha said she wanted to talk to the custody sergeant before seeing Imelda. To her relief it was Aaron Brown, a man she knew well and, most importantly, someone whose assessment of character she trusted well. Given he dealt with a lot of bad apples, he could still pick out the really bad ones.

As he spotted Martha and Krisha walking towards him, his expression grew serious. "I'm hearing I have you two to thank for bringing Imelda Taylor into my life."

"I take it you share our view that she's a wrong 'un," said Martha.

"That'll do for starters," said Aaron. He was a man famed for his laid-back manner and ability to defuse the tensest of situations.

"How about vicious, dangerous and unpredictable?" he added.

"So, you're not thinking she's a slightly batty cat lady."

"Any sensible cat would run a mile."

"I take it she kept up that weird smirking."

"And the even weirder laughing."

"That's new. What was that about?"

"When I read out the grounds for her arrest, she seemed to find it amusing to be accused of killing so many people. I'm not easily swayed but she left me unsettled. It felt like she was watching me in the way a panther watches a deer."

"Thanks for the warning," said Martha. "I can see we might need medical assistance."

"I thought you might go down that path." He pulled a sheet of paper from his top pocket and handed it to her. "That's the name and telephone number of one of the most sensible shrinks we have on call."

"You're a top man, Aaron." Before she could say anymore there was a commotion as a youngish man, under the influence of drink, drugs or both, was brought towards the sergeant. He sighed and wished them luck before reluctantly engaging with the new arrival.

As they walked off, they could hear the man being asked for his name.

"Mickey Fucking Mouse," came the reply.

"Don't tell me," they heard the custody sergeant say, "you live in Disney Land, Florida, which makes Brixton a long way from home."

They walked on, the sound of talking fading behind as they approached the interview room where Imelda was being held. Martha was first through the door. It was a case of déjà vu. Imelda was sitting with her hands flat on the table, her eyes looking vacant as she stared into the middle distance. The smirk was still there. If anything, it was even more pronounced.

Martha felt her temper rising and looked away. She was not going to give this woman the pleasure of seeing her lose control. She sat directly opposite, with Krisha taking the next seat. A uniformed PC was standing against the rear wall, managing to be both present and discreet.

No one spoke. No one moved. Then Imelda's eyes focused on her immediate surroundings. It felt uncannily like she had just entered the room. Martha waited; she sensed it was important to get Imelda to talk first.

Imelda's eyes drifted slowly towards Krisha, carefully looking her up and down, repeating the process three times. Finally, she shook her head before turning the full force of her gaze on Martha. As before, her brown eyes moved up and down three times, then she stopped, took her hands off the table and steepled her fingers in front of her face.

"You must be her . . . Martha. He told me what you looked like."

Martha put so much effort into not responding she was surprised she didn't give herself a hernia.

The waiting became more intense but still Martha refused to speak. It was Imelda who finally spoke, her voice surprisingly gentle, but the words hit Martha with the force of a slap in the face.

"Neil Thompson sends his regards."

CHAPTER 42

"There's good news and bad news. Which would you prefer?" Harry said, placing a mug of steaming tea in front of Julie to go with the plate of bacon rolls he'd already handed over. She'd liberally dosed hers with brown sauce.

Julie looked at her food then at Harry. The bacon won. She held up her left hand while using her right to grab a roll. It disappeared in double-quick time.

"How can something that tastes so good be bad for you?" she said, before resisting the second round to answer Harry's question.

"Let's hear some good news. I like good news."

Harry looked a little apologetic. "I was being a bit tricksy there. I should have said that the good news leads into bad news, so it could be said to be all bad news."

Julie decided to contemplate this over her second roll. She finished and wiped her fingers on a paper towel.

"Why don't you just give me the news?"

They were sitting in the kitchen of Martha's home in Idmiston Road, West Dulwich. It was at the back of the three-bedroomed property, and double doors opened onto a small courtyard garden. It was a warm day in early spring and the garden was full of butterflies.

Harry leaned back and closed his eyes, like he was hoping some form of inspiration would strike. For some reason his gesture struck Julie as ominous. She didn't want to know what he had to say. But of course, she would listen. If it was news about a threat to her friend Martha or, even worse, a threat against Martha's daughter, Betty, she had to know. How was she going to help if she didn't know what was going on.

Harry was sitting straight again. "There's no way of sugar-coating this. It's about Neil Thompson."

It might have been tempting to say you could hear a pin drop in the ensuing silence, but actually what you would have heard is one of Julie's hands thumping down on the table in rage.

"That weasel, that bastard. No doubt hiding in the shadows like the coward he is. I'd like to place my hands round his neck and squeeze until his eyeballs popped out."

Julie was a woman who always spoke her mind. Despite his mounting worries, Harry couldn't keep a wry smile off his face. With Julie there was never any question of explaining what her role was. She was big, strong, fearless and loyal to her friends. But the thing which impressed him most was her bold use of colour. Today she was sporting bright orange hair, yesterday it had been green and purple, tomorrow it might be pink. It was not a look he would be able to recreate any time soon, given their fifty-year age gap. The best he could aspire to was the polished look. Hair or no hair, they saw eye to eye on most things, chief among them a willingness to risk their lives in protecting Martha.

"You said something about good and bad news?"

"Er, well . . ." Harry looked bashful. "I was trying to put a bit of spin on everything. I thought it might put you off your lunch if I gave it you all in one go."

"Harry, for God's sake, spit it out. I'm a big girl and you're a big boy. Trying to put a spin on it ain't going to make things any better."

"You're right, of course. Well, the news is that Neil Thompson may not be his real name."

"OK," said Julie drawing out the word. "Unsurprising. A tricky bastard like him *would* have different identities. But something tells me you've got more."

"Yup," said Harry, allowing some of the anger he was feeling to show on his face, reminding Julie why her friend had earned such a fearsome reputation as a gangland enforcer.

Harry clenched his fists. "Before you ask, I have no idea what his real name is, but I've saved the real doozie to the end. In fact, you could say it's two real doozies. First, if we didn't think he was slippery enough already, it turns out he may have political connections."

Julie opened her mouth to ask a question, but Harry kept on speaking.

"I know what you're going to say, and the answer is, all I have are some suggestions from people who know about these things. His connections might not even be here in the UK, it could be anywhere. We're talking about a man who's involved in crime all over the world — people trafficking, drugs, software piracy . . . the list goes on."

"You mean he could be working with anyone, from people on our side to . . . take your pick. It could be the Russians, Chinese, even the Americans."

"That might be the case, and that would be bad enough," said Harry. "But the second thing might turn out to be even more crucial."

"This is giving me goosebumps, Harry. What could be worse?"

"He might be able to be in different places at the same time."

"Harry!" said an exasperated Julie. "What are you talking about?"

"It's complicated, so stay with me. One of my contacts came up with a very strange comment. He said, and I quote, 'He likes to keep things close, very close.'

"Now, I've been trying to make sense of that ever since, then I remembered something. Martha's dad once told me there was a large family, all dedicated to crime. Only blood relations can make it to the top of this tree. No outsiders."

"Come on, Harry," said Julie, looking impatient. "There's plenty of crime families about. What's so special about one more?"

"What if this crime family all had jobs at the Met?"

"Surely they'd stand out," said Julie.

"That is a fair comment," said Harry. "But I was wondering, what if there's someone on Martha's current team who's related to this 'Neil Thompson'," he said, indicating quotation marks around the name.

Julie felt an urge to stand up, channelling her restless energy into the mundane task of making more tea. As she carefully poured freshly boiled water over a teabag in each mug, she said, "I can see why you wanted to dress things up. I was worried before, but now I'm terrified. So, unless you have some other plan for me, I'm going to drink this cup of tea, very quickly, and head out to Betty's school. That little girl is not being let out of my sight until we get Neil Thompson, or whatever his name is."

"I wish you could do the same with Martha," said Harry. "I'd be far happier if I could hide them both away."

"I think we can keep Betty safely under wraps," replied Julie. "But her mum? You don't need me to tell you that she will not react well to any suggestion that she goes into hiding."

"You're right, of course you are. One of us needs to get a message to her that we need to talk very soon. In the meantime, she'll be delighted you have Betty." He looked thoughtful. "Everything is happening so fast; we haven't spoken to Betty's dad yet. Better do that pronto so he can come straight home."

"I agree, but even two days ago there was no sense any of this might be a threat to Martha and her family. Make sure you tell Justin I have her."

"Will do. He's over in the US — Nevada, I think. I'll bell him later on this afternoon."

Harry's mobile rang. It was Martha. Raising his eyebrows, he showed Julie the caller ID then answered.

"Martha, we need to talk as soon as you can. It's about our friend."

"I was calling to say the same thing. I should be able to get home by eight tonight. More importantly, is Betty OK?"

"Julie's on the case. We'll get her home and keep her safe."

* * *

On the other end of the line Martha was hit by a wave of emotion. Knowing Harry and Julie were looking out for Betty meant more than she could say.

"Thanks Harry," she managed, after regaining her composure. "Am I right in thinking that I may not like what you have to say?"

The brief silence was telling; it stiffened Martha's resolve. Promising to call Harry regularly, she walked back towards the interview room, where she had left Krisha observing Imelda.

"Anything new?"

Krisha nodded. "Apparently, we have a lawyer on the way to represent Imelda. He should be here very soon, according to the message. How do you want to play it?"

"That was pretty fast work to get a lawyer here. Someone's well connected." She looked at Imelda, who had resumed her earlier pose, hands flat on the table and smirk firmly in place. Martha felt a rising sense of concern. Imelda's strange performance, the Neil Thompson comment and now this lawyer turning up out of the blue — it felt like someone was looking over her shoulder.

She glanced at Martha and noted her appraising expression, a look which said, *It's time you came clean with me.* Martha decided it was now or never.

"Shall we go and grab a coffee while we wait?"

In the event Martha didn't need to find a way into what she feared might be a difficult conversation; Krisha beat her to it. They were walking up the busy Brixton High Street heading for a coffee shop when she touched her lightly on the arm.

"Permission to speak freely, ma'am?"

"You never need my permission, and less of the ma'am, please. Tell me what's on your mind."

"In that case," said Krisha, "why do I get the feeling that something's going on, and who is Neil Thompson? When Imelda came out with his name you went white as a sheet."

They'd both come to stop and were facing each other on the pavement as people bustled past. Krisha could see her words had struck a chord.

"Look, if you don't want to tell me I'll understand, but I think it would be a mistake. It obviously has something to do with this case and I'm certain I can help you. Even if it's just to shoulder some of the pressure — you know, a problem shared and all that."

Martha felt her eyes prickling with sudden emotion. She blinked a few times and took a few breaths to restore her equilibrium.

"It's a long story," she said.

"Then the sooner you get started, the sooner you'll finish."

CHAPTER 43

Coffees in hand, Martha and Krisha were now in an unused interview room, with the warning from the custody sergeant they might get kicked out.

"If we can get five minutes that'll be great," said Martha. "As soon as Imelda's lawyer arrives, we want to get back to interviewing her."

Part of her wanted to run home to see Betty. A bigger part said she needed to find out as much as possible because information was key. Could Imelda lead her to Neil Thompson?

Martha took a sip of the hot latte as she assembled her thoughts. Considering she'd been dreading this moment, she felt calm. It helped that Krisha was so clearly a decent woman who would give her a fair hearing.

"Look, I know I should have briefed you before, but I really wasn't sure about things until recently," she said.

"Thank you for not saying it was 'complicated'," said Krisha. "My partner told me it was complicated when I caught her kissing another girl."

Martha looked rueful. "I'm glad I decided to be careful, although the truth is the whole story is complicated . . . too complicated to tell in the time we've got. So, I was going to suggest that, if we can somehow find the time, you come over to my place, meet my friends and we tell you what we know."

"Sounds good to me, but it would be good to hear the highlights."

"OK," said Martha. "A bit of history first. There's a man I know of as Neil Thompson. He hides in the background, has major criminal connections including all types of trafficking from people, drugs, money . . . you name it. His existence was discovered by my father, and this is where it gets complicated.

"You know my dad was an anti-corruption cop. Well, he found out about Thompson because he was bribing so many police officers. For some reason Dad kept quiet about it. I don't know why that is, but I live in hope that he was trying to set this Neil Thompson up to arrest him." That unreadable expression from before flashed across her face. "My dad died before he could get this man, and cutting a very long story short, it turns out this master criminal, with global connections, thinks my dad left me some sort of secret diary detailing all he knew about Thompson and the people he'd corrupted."

Martha stared intently at Krisha. "If I tell you the next bit, you get sucked a little further into something that isn't really your problem."

"Oh, don't worry about that. You had me hooked when you mentioned fighting corrupt officers. I can't think of anything worse than a bent copper." Krisha spoke with a fierceness that mirrored Martha's.

"You took the words right out of my mouth," said Martha. "The really big secret is that I *do* have part of a diary — but it's in code. We've managed to work out some of the names — all people long retired — so I'm not sure what its true value is. It all feels like ancient history. I've been thinking hard, and I don't see what could possibly have induced this killing spree, especially as the victims have no connection to this at all. I handed the diary over to a woman called Carol. She once worked with my father and promised to keep it safe. She has her own reasons for keeping it out of sight."

They both lapsed into silence, trying to find a way through the maze.

"Unless . . ." began Krisha, a spark of energy forming.

"Unless there's something I don't know?" said Martha.

"Well, it's definitely something you don't know. It's just a matter of working out what it is."

Both women fell silent again, then Martha carried on explaining why she had kept such potentially momentous news to herself.

"Right up to today, I was hoping and praying that he had moved on. I didn't hear anything for months. Then I was somehow put on the case of the missing cats and, as you know, that rapidly escalated to murder."

"You got the sense that Thompson was behind it all," confirmed Krisha.

"I did because it started in such a weird way then got worse. He's a man who's grown so used to manipulating people to get his own way that he's addicted to playing mind games. I think he gets a real thrill out of it. One of the hallmarks of his machinations is the way he almost overengineers his plots. He loves misdirection and creating confusion. I suspect the murders in Dulwich were his way of drawing in police time and resources. As he knows full well, we can hardly put this investigation to one side, so that gives him the perfect time to move on to the next phase.

"When Imelda came out with her 'Neil Thompson sends his regards' stuff it confirmed my worst fears, my living nightmare. This is a man who was responsible for the murder of my mother and the abduction of my little girl."

Her eyes were bright, and she wiped them fiercely with her hands.

"I also heard he was responsible for you being sent to prison," said Krisha, becoming emotional herself.

"That's the least of my worries," said Martha, waving the idea away. "The point is I should have filled you in right at the start, but I didn't. I wasn't trying to keep things from you. I think partly I didn't want it to be true, so I think I convinced myself that not talking about it would make it go away."

Krisha looked at Martha kindly, like someone she was already regarding as a friend. "I totally understand. I would probably have done the same. Can I ask one question, and feel free to tell me it's none of my business."

Martha kept silent but nodded yes.

"Do you think you should report this? Get the Met behind you?"

"I've thought about that almost constantly. The trouble is I don't know who Thompson has bribed. He's a very wealthy man who's not afraid to splash his money around. He also has contacts everywhere, not just the police. I know for a fact he has people in the legal system, politics and business. He's got tentacles everywhere."

"But even so, wouldn't your family be safer under police guard? Or are you saying that's a risk too?"

"I don't know," said Martha. "It's one of the awful things about corruption, you start suspecting everyone. Truth and trust go out of the window.

"But with my friends, at least I can be sure my daughter, Betty, is very well protected. That's why I've suggested you come round and meet the team. They're lovely people but you wouldn't want to annoy them."

"I'd heard you were one of the fiercest, most independent coppers around. I was already thinking you were pretty impressive, but a back story like that . . . I can't wait to meet Team Martha, they sound very special."

Any more conversation was cut off as a uniformed officer opened the door.

"Your suspect's lawyer is here."

CHAPTER 44

Imelda's lawyer was a small, neat woman, dressed very conservatively in a dark trouser suit and sporting an old-fashioned pearl necklace with matching earrings. She had minimal makeup and dark red lipstick. The only thing missing from the retro look was a pair of horn-rimmed glasses. She gazed unblinkingly at Martha and Krisha as they sat down. Imelda was somehow managing to look smugger than ever.

She introduced herself as Liz Grainger, senior partner at Mayhew and Black, a famously expensive and fearsome law firm. Martha raised an eyebrow and shared a look with Krisha. There was only one way someone like Imelda could have such a high-powered lawyer: Neil Thompson was paying for it.

"If I may make some observations? It might help." The lawyer had a surprisingly deep voice, but it was clear she wasn't really asking a question, but making a statement of intent. Martha inclined her head in a gesture of consent.

"Well then, I'm glad we see eye to eye."

"I wouldn't assume we see things the same way at all," said Martha.

Grainger's face darkened and for a moment it looked like she might lose her temper, but the next moment she was firmly back in control.

"Perhaps you're right," she said. "But I wouldn't be so certain of that. Because unless you're a mind reader, I think I will be presenting you with some startling information."

Martha had no idea how to respond to that, so kept quiet.

"As I suspected," said Grainger, her face taking on an arch expression.

"But first a question: has my client been medically assessed yet, as I suspect there are strong grounds to say that mental incapacity renders her unfit for this process."

"I'm going to take a wild guess here and say that you're talking about her dead mother?" said Martha. "Well, there's a doctor on the way, and he's aware of the circumstances."

"I doubt he is aware. At least not of the full picture — just the small amount you've managed to pass on to him."

She reached into her bag and produced an iPad, which she took her time setting up. Martha and Krisha waited patiently — acting deliberately slowly was one of the oldest tricks in the book, and falling for it would be a rookie mistake. Eventually she seemed happy with her efforts, having teed up a video so that it was paused on a shot of Imelda looking into a camera. She positioned the iPad so that they could all see it.

"I think you will find the clip I am about to play most instructive. I will of course make it available to you."

She hit play, and all four people, even the apparently oblivious Imelda, leaned in to get a closer look. The sound and picture quality were clear. The camera pulled back to show Imelda sitting in a chair, with her clearly dead mother sitting in a chair beside her. Grainger paused the video.

"This was shot in the flat she shared with her mother."

The video resumed and showed Imelda turning to her left as she spoke. "Did you read about the one who got his head chopped off? You should have been there. The blood went everywhere."

There was a pause while she apparently listened to a reply.

"I got the idea when I was watching that woman on TikTok."

Another pause as she turned sideways, her head slightly inclined as if she was listening to her mother. Then she nodded.

"TikTok is like Facebook, only better."

Another pause. This time she appeared to listen intently before a sharp shake of the head.

"No, he didn't say anything. His head flew through the air. It made me laugh, to be honest. Silly old git, he should have been looking where he was going."

Grainger stopped the video again.

"There's plenty more like that. Perhaps now you see why I said I doubted your doctor was anywhere near being well enough informed. I also suspect he lacks the qualifications to make a correct diagnosis. It's why I've asked an eminent professor of psychiatry to examine Imelda. I don't know what you think, but from what we've seen so far, this young lady needs special care and attention. I'm sure my client won't mind me saying that she's a troubled young woman. It may be that even now she doesn't realise her mother is dead."

Three pairs of eyes turned towards Imelda, who was showing no reaction to the conversation. If anything, she seemed even more detached from the proceedings. Martha felt her heart sink. It was clear Imelda was experiencing some form of mental health crisis, and it was likely that she might avoid being held accountable for her crimes. Despite her gloom she refused to give in at the first hurdle.

"May I ask how you obtained this recording?"

"Of course, I was waiting for you to ask. I have several recordings to show you — one is quite startling — and they came as attachments to the email instructing us to take on Imelda as a client."

"What about a name on the email?"

"Not much help to you there, I'm afraid. It was sent by a partner in a Bahamian firm, who was paid by another offshore company with no means of contact. You're welcome to try and follow the trail, but it will get you nowhere.

"Now, let me show you something really interesting."

CHAPTER 45

Harry's phone rang as he was pouring freshly boiled water into a large teapot. Seeing it was Julie calling, he instantly put the kettle down and picked up the phone.

"What's up?"

"I think there may be some of Thompson's people down by the school," she said, her voice tense.

"You're sure?"

"If anyone else asked me that I'd deck 'em . . . Yes. There's two of them and they're watching the route we use when we walk home."

"Just checking . . . OK. I'm on my way now. How good do you think they are?"

"I could probably deal with both of them, but why take the risk? Especially with Betty around. What about the house, you'll be leaving it unguarded?"

"I've got some of the local talent keeping an eye. They're not the toughest, but they can take care of an empty house for a short while. Are you tooling up?"

"I've got a bit of mace. Nothing like a shot of pepper spray to the face to keep people honest."

"Look, everyone down at the school knows you. Can you tell them Betty needs to leave half an hour early for a dental appointment? You can say it was my fault for for-getting it and I just called you." Harry stepped outside and pulled the front door closed behind him. "I'm on my way. Tell me what to watch out for."

"There's two of them near the junction of Rosendale Road and the South Circular. They're both in jeans and T-shirts, short hair and one has a full sleeve of tattoos on his right arm. They're about mid-twenties and look like they're regulars at the gym."

"I'll keep an eye out for them," said Harry. "When I get to you let's decide whether to go on the front foot or wait for them to make a move."

"Personally, I prefer punching first and asking questions later." A malicious laugh floated out of Harry's speaker. "See you shortly," said Harry, breaking the connection.

He nodded at the two men keeping a watch on Martha's house and set off at a fast pace that belied his seventy-five years. Harry had always kept himself fit, and saw no reason to stop now he was getting older.

As he walked towards the school, he spotted the two men Julie had told him about. Looking at them, he saw why Julie felt they were lightweights. They had the tone you get from lifting weights, but Harry had street-fighting skills that were second to none. He doubted these two would survive sixty seconds. He was tempted to deal with them on the spot but decided to wait. No need to create a ruckus before prop-erly assessing the situation.

Julie was waiting inside the entrance. "Did you see them? All muscles and sharp clothes. They're so obvious I wonder if they're a distraction."

"The same thought occurred to me. It seems a bit strange," said Harry, flexing his fingers on both hands. He'd once told Julie it was the only bit of warming up he ever did. "Have you seen anyone else?"

"No," she said, her expression intense. "And I have been looking . . . believe me."

"In that case, why don't I chase off those two and you stay here and wait for Betty. I take it the school is fine about letting her go early?"

"Yes, and yes," said Julie. "Although I wouldn't mind chatting to our new friends." The prospect of action was making her bounce lightly on her toes.

"I think you might frighten them too much," said Harry, his face creasing in a smile. "I wonder what the charge is for scaring someone to death?"

"I can't be blamed if they have weak constitutions," said Julie, who was wearing an especially sinister grin and now almost dancing on the spot.

"I hate to burst your bubble," said Harry. "But I think it has to be me. You're well known at the school, whereas I'm another old git who's wandered in off the street."

He paused and Julie remained silent.

"You might have said I'm not an old git . . . Anyway, I'll be back in a minute."

Harry walked up to the traffic lights and while he waited, he made eye contact with his two targets. His expression was not friendly, and the pair looked uncomfortable. By the time the walk signal went green they were close to cracking. Seeing Harry jogging over the crossing was the final straw and the two bolted in the direction of Tulse Hill, not slowing down as they vanished from view.

Harry turned and saw Julie standing outside. He spread his arms wide in a "What can you do?" gesture. When he got back to Julie, she narrowed her eyes at him in mock anger. "Seems like I'm not the only one who's a bit too scary for their own good."

"This gets weirder," said Harry. "As soon as you have Betty, let's get out of here. I take it you still haven't spotted anyone else."

Julie shook her head, leaving Harry with a growing sense of unease. It was time to step up his work on sweating his contacts. Although many had retired, enough remained active to be helpful. Up to now he'd been probing quite gently, but it was time to go full steam ahead. Events were coming to the boil.

* * *

Less than a mile away, a dirty white panel van pulled up outside a locked door into the now disused police station on Lordship Lane, East Dulwich. The rear doors of the van opened and a man with bolt cutters sliced through the large padlocks on the door and the three men were quickly inside. Armed with lump hammers they knew exactly where they were heading, a former office on the ground floor of the dusty and dry smelling building.

Entering the room, they quickly set about knocking holes in the plasterboard until one of the men called out, "Got it." He reached inside the ragged hole he'd made and pulled out a metal box about the size of a large novel. It was locked shut. The man looked at his leader who nodded. Using a small crowbar, the lid was prised open and only then was it handed to the leader. Looking inside, a tight smile — which never reached his eyes — flashed briefly on to his face. Then, he turned and jogged back to the waiting van followed by the other two. Doors slammed shut, the van moved off, soon swallowed up in the press of traffic. The whole thing had taken less than three minutes, while the fastest police responder was still two minutes away. In the ongoing struggle that was crime-fighting in London, this was low priority.

CHAPTER 46

The next video was cued up. Now Imelda was sitting on the end of her bed looking at a laptop. With the picture frozen it was hard to see what was holding her attention.

"I believe this is taken in Imelda's bedroom in the flat she shared with her mother," said Grainger. She went to hit the play button, but Martha stopped her with a raised hand. "Was there a third person in the flat to take the video?"

"Ah, yes," said Grainger, giving a not terribly convincing impression that she had just remembered something. "I forgot. In the instruction there is a small section explaining the pictures were taken using military-grade surveillance systems — the technology is top secret and, I understand, can be operated remotely and is virtually undetectable. Little wonder your SOCOs missed it."

As the lawyer finished talking, Krisha and Martha exchanged a look before Krisha got to her feet. "I'll let the crime scene manager know there's something to look for, and it sounds like we may need to bring in some outside expertise to examine what we find."

Martha watched Krisha pull the door shut behind her, then she turned her attention back to Grainger. There seemed little point in looking at Imelda, who was still in a trance-like state. Plus, that annoying smirk was still on display.

"If you don't mind, I'd like to briefly suspend the interview while we wait for my colleague to return," said Martha. "I hadn't anticipated that we would need to search for top-secret surveillance equipment."

The lawyer shrugged in acceptance.

Martha maintained a determinedly professional outlook. "Anyone need to go to the toilet while we wait? Or perhaps a drink?" When no answer was forthcoming, she made her own way out of the room. She was glad of the chance to think, having the strongest sense that the investigation was about to become even murkier. The other side would only offer up fresh information if it was to their advantage. She texted Krisha: *Meet me in the canteen when you're done. We need to exchange ideas.*

CHAPTER 47

Martha refused to budge despite the protests from Julie and Harry, who wanted to go on the offensive the moment she told them of Imelda's message from Thompson.

"She said what?" demanded an angry Harry, who together with Julie, insisted Martha run through the day's developments for a second time. After Martha repeated herself, they both looked shocked. "We have to do something," said Julie. "We can't let this ride."

"Where do we go? Who do we go after?" said Martha. "He has a big advantage — he knows all about us, we know next to nothing about him. I'm all in favour of knocking ten bells out of him, but we can't if we don't even know what he looks like, or where he is."

Julie sighed with exasperation. "We have to do something."

"Which we are," said Martha, sounding a lot calmer than she felt as she patted her friend on the arm. "What we're going to do is keep on looking for information that levels the playing field."

* * *

The following morning Harry was approaching a large, detached house in Tadworth, Surrey — an attractive

185

red-brick property of the type which said the people who lived here had done well for themselves. The front entrance was flanked by large windows on either side, and there were gleaming new cars on the driveway — a Mercedes convertible and a huge Range Rover that looked to be lacking nothing in extras. Harry, who was not easily impressed by motor cars, recognised that the two he was looking at were worth a small fortune. The Merc had one of those AMG badges which he knew marked it as a top-of-the-range model, while the Range Rover was called an Autobiography, which put the car in the 'if you need to ask the price you can't afford it' category.

While it didn't impress Harry, it did confirm one thing: there was something dodgy about the man who lived there, former Met Police Detective Sergeant Roger Edwards. The man who had taken such delight in tormenting Martha until his sudden and unexpected retirement.

Harry did the sums. Those two cars alone would have cost low six figures, while the house, in this part of Surrey, was going to be more than a million pounds. Not a bad little nest egg for a man now living on a police pension. Harry knew the ex-sergeant had some explaining to do. Either he'd got lucky on the stock market, won the lottery, come into an inheritance — or maybe his wife was very successful. Harry already knew his wife worked part time as a physiotherapist so doubted it was down to the last option. The truth was Sergeant Edwards was a corrupt little git who owed his fortune to taking back-handers from people like Neil Thompson. At least that was Harry's view, and he was here today to remind the dodgy cop that there was no such thing as a free lunch.

Harry had been given this address last night while Martha was still at Brixton with Imelda Taylor. Not wanting to waste any time he'd already decided to act, even before Martha gave the plan her blessing. He hoped that today would be a chance to add a little background to their enemy, and even more important, find out why the man who called himself Neil Thompson was pursuing her at all.

Obviously, it had something to do with her father, but she was at a loss to know what. He agreed with her dismissal of the idea that it had something to do with the secret diary. She speculated that he believed she had another coded book, and although she didn't, her father had loved his little tricks and feints. She couldn't entirely rule out that her ultra-secretive dad had another book hidden away.

She had decided the only option was to try and open a dialogue with Thompson directly, tell him she didn't have anything on him and hope he accepted her word.

Harry had hated the idea from the moment Martha came up with it; the thought of trying to negotiate with such a slippery customer left him cold. He felt Thompson was a man who lived in a world of lies, and trying to appeal to his better nature would be an impossible task. Plus, how did they reach him? They could hardly call him up. But Martha was determined, and that explained why Harry was now standing on the driveway of Edwards' house, pumped up and ready for a confrontation. Harry doubted that a lowlife like Edwards would have any direct dealings with Thompson, but he must have someone he reported to, who in turn would be able to pass a message upwards.

There was no point in hanging around. Putting on a small face mask — it wasn't much but enough to befuddle security cameras — he marched up the drive and was pleasantly surprised to find that Edwards favoured an old-school buzzer, not one of those internet-connected devices with a built-in speaker and camera. Removing the mask, he pressed the button. It was loud, so he was sure it would be heard. Sure enough, after a short wait, the door opened, and he laid eyes on his prey. He was unimpressed. Despite it being a cool day, Edwards looked short, fat and sweaty, with a shiny forehead that badly needed mopping with a cloth.

He demonstrated the charm which had so impressed Martha.

"If you're some sort of vagrant looking for a handout, you can fuck off. The Salvation Army's down the road, they look after useless old gits like you."

Harry rubbed his hands together and tried to look as harmless as possible. "Could you manage a sandwich for an old soldier?"

"My wife does all that sort of thing," said Edwards with a smug little grin. "But she's out, and even if she was here, I wouldn't let her make you anything. Now, I won't tell you again — clear off, you dirty little scrote. And have a wash, you stink."

Had he been paying attention, Edwards might have noticed Harry's little nod as he confirmed his target was home alone, but as Martha had told him, thinking wasn't the man's strong point. What he saw standing on his doorstep was a stooped, elderly man dressed in ragged clothing, someone down on his luck. He also failed to notice Harry was wearing surgical gloves. Even as Edwards' words were ringing in his ears, Harry had surreptitiously looked around to check none of the neighbours were looking. All was quiet, not even a net curtain twitched.

With the coast clear, Harry moved fast. Using both hands, he gripped Edwards under the armpits and lifted him straight off the ground before marching his victim back into the house, then kicked the front door firmly shut. Edwards had gone from a bright red colour to a nasty shade of grey. He was sweating more than ever as his predicament hit home. If it came to a fight, he was seriously outgunned and wouldn't stand a chance. Harry put him back on the ground, then held up a gloved finger and mimed a shushing gesture. Now Edwards noted the gloves and the implication hit him. This man meant business and didn't intend to leave many clues behind.

Harry took a painful grip of his jaw with his left hand, while producing a knife with his right. He pressed the blade hard enough against Edwards' throat to draw a thin line of blood.

Edwards made to cry out in fear, but the powerful grip on his jaw silenced him. He started whimpering as his bladder released. Harry didn't bother to acknowledge it had happened. People wetting themselves was nothing. He'd once induced a heart attack in one man just by threatening him. Right now, he looked an entirely different proposition to the kindly older man who could often be found holding Betty's hand as he walked her down to school. Taking care to avoid the pool of urine, he kept up the pressure on Edwards' jaw for a few seconds more, then with shocking speed he banged his head against the wall three times in succession. Edwards briefly blacked out before coming round again.

"Please, if it's money you want, I've got £20,000 in cash in my safe." Speaking appeared painful now. His tongue had swollen, making it stick to the roof of his mouth — he sounded like a drunk at the end of a long session.

"Money's not going to help you," said Harry. The words came out slowly and each one was emphasised with a firm bang of his head against the wall. He started to go green, and Harry moved fast to let him go as his knees buckled and he vomited down his shirt front.

"Who's the dirty little scrote now?" Harry showed his sympathy with a sharp kick in the groin. Edwards groaned out loud and retched painfully, clutching his nether regions.

Watching him intently, Harry judged his prey was coming round after toying with the idea of losing consciousness. Seeing Edwards was back in the land of the living, he placed his size-twelve foot against Edwards' groin and pressed firmly.

It had the desired effect as his victim went still and stopped whimpering.

"No more, please. I have a bad heart. What do you want?"

"I want everything you've got on Neil Thompson. And don't go talking bollocks and saying you've never heard of him."

Despite this, the faintest hint of defiance emerged. Harry raised his foot and slammed it down into Edwards' groin.

Two minutes later the ex-detective was begging to be given a chance to talk.

"I haven't got much, I don't talk to him directly," said Edwards. "I report to my contact. I don't know if he talks to

Thompson or someone else. All I know is that eventually my contact lets me know what he wants me to do."

Harry made a growling noise and pressed his foot more firmly.

"On my wife's life," said Edwards, his voice climbing until the words came out as a high-pitched squeak. "Don't hurt me, I'm trying to tell you everything I know. I did meet him once. He was a psycho, threatened to make me eat my own bollocks if I let him down. Until you showed up, I've never met a more frightening man."

Edwards went silent, so Harry waggled his foot.

"Wait, wait. I have got something, something you will be interested in."

Harry lifted his foot.

"Talk to me."

"I can do better than that — I can show you."

CHAPTER 48

Krisha walked into the busy canteen and picked out Martha, who'd managed to find a table in the corner. She had it to herself, thanks to the fierce glare she directed at all who came near.

As she sat down Martha pushed a mug of tea in her direction. "I'm not hungry and you eat less than me, so I didn't bother with food."

"Good. I don't know about you, but there's something about being in the same space as Imelda that makes me lose my appetite. I couldn't bear the thought of being her brief and actually having to defend her."

"You and me both," said Martha. "I'm not unhappy about taking a break right now. I could do with a chance to compose myself before we go on."

"What do you think this surveillance footage is going to show? When I told the crime scene manager they had to go back and find super-secret gear she looked at me like I'd gone mad and muttered something about James Bond."

"But she's going back?" said Martha.

"Oh, you needn't worry about that. I told her if she thought I was Bond then she should meet my boss. I said you're in a bad mood and itching to go all Blofeld on someone's arse."

"You didn't?" said Martha unable to suppress a snort of laughter.

"I did, and she actually curtsied."

She quickly became serious again. "Sounds like we may have some very high-tech, eyes-only gear on our hands soon. What do you think we should do about it?"

"I've been wondering about that," said Martha. "I don't want to put any noses out of shape, but it may be gear that our lot aren't familiar with. I'm thinking we might need to involve GCHQ. I know they hate it when the spooks get involved, but we may have no choice."

She glanced around, double-checking there was no one within hearing range. Satisfied, she carried on. "Let's not get ahead of ourselves. The first thing is to find out what information has been recorded and understand why Imelda's lawyer was so keen to bring it to our attention."

"You're right, of course," said Krisha. "I get a bit carried away with tech, always have. That lawyer is just trying to confuse things."

"The thought had crossed my mind."

"What could possibly get Imelda off the hook?" asked Krisha.

"I imagine her mental state is going to come up," said Martha. "Let's face it, spending all that time with her dead mother doesn't speak highly for her sanity. I can't see how the lawyer can help but play the 'diminished responsibility' card."

"I fear you're right," said Krisha. "But forgive me being cynical — she started her killing before her mum died."

"I couldn't agree more," said Martha as she checked the time. They'd left the interview room twenty minutes earlier and it was time to get back. She drained her tea, smoothed her front and looked at Krisha. "Ready to conquer the world?"

"You lead, I'll follow."

CHAPTER 49

Harry couldn't recall the last time he had enjoyed himself so much. He was smiling as he strode back to his car, which he'd taken the precaution of parking a good mile away to avoid unwanted attention. He kept up a fast pace as he went over what had happened. Getting the chance to beat the snot out of the fat little git who'd made Martha's life miserable was worth it in its own right, but even better, he'd learned something that might prove invaluable.

He'd left Edwards in little doubt that if he talked out of turn then Harry would be back, "and next time you really won't like what happens to you". He knew he sounded like a character in a B-movie, but it had the desired effect, making the retired policeman tremble even more.

To ram the message home, Harry had made to leave then stopped and grabbed Edwards' head between his two huge hands. At first the man tried to struggle, but as the pressure on his head increased, he slowly became still, breathing heavily through his now forcibly pursed lips. Harry almost laughed: Edwards literally looked like a fish out of water.

"You might be able to redeem yourself by delivering a message, but not until I tell you. In the meantime, don't go talking to anyone, especially not anyone connected to Neil

Thompson. And don't go thinking your old mates will help you. If I can't get to you on the outside then I'll wait until you end up inside — we've got enough on you to have you put away for a long time, and you'll find prison is no safer. It might be even worse."

All the time he was talking, Harry never once lost eye contact, and Edwards knew that he would never be able to forget the frightening coldness he saw reflected back at him. Letting him go, Harry added, "Don't bother answering. You're either bright enough to get it or you're dead."

He let go of the man's head and watched as he slid to the ground, ending up sitting in his own piss and sick. It was where he belonged. As Harry walked away, he forgot all about the corrupt cop. He had bigger fish to fry.

CHAPTER 50

The break had lasted less than half an hour, but there was a subtle difference in the atmosphere of the interview room. The change of mood did not make Martha more confident. Grainger, the lawyer, was leaning back in her chair attempting to look nonchalant, but even her hooded eyes were unable to hide her excitement at what was coming next. She had the air of a defence lawyer who was about to play her best card.

With a grimace, Martha switched to Imelda to see if she could pick up any clues. Again, she didn't like what she saw. Imelda had lost the smirk and was now staring into the middle distance, but this time Martha had the strongest sense that she was just biding her time and paying far more attention than her attitude might indicate.

Martha turned away from the two women and looked at Krisha, who she judged was feeling the same way. She decided the best thing was to buy time, test the other side's patience. She glanced at the uniformed officer standing over to one side. "Do you need a break, officer?" she asked, hoping he would say yes. Unfortunately, her powers of telepathy failed as the PC politely informed her he was doing fine.

Not to be deterred, she looked at Grainger. "What about you and Imelda? Have you had drinks and toilet breaks?

These are very serious allegations, so I'm happy to take all the time you need." She added a big, bright smile which Harry and Julie always told her was exceptionally irritating. "No one can look that happy and really mean it," Harry had once told her.

To her disappointment, her little ploy failed to gain any traction at all. If anything, she thought the lawyer was looking at her with some mirth. She took a deep breath. Time to move on. If she went too far down this path, she was in danger of losing focus. "Well, if everyone's happy, let's . . ."

Grainger surprised her by sitting up straight and holding her right hand up, palm out. It seemed the lawyer also had a few little tricks of her own.

Martha waited slightly longer than necessary as she found herself being drawn into a power play over who controlled the interview, then chided herself for falling into such an obvious trap.

She looked at the lawyer, her face a mask of inscrutable professionalism.

"I do apologise. Please, you have the floor." She made a sweeping gesture with her right hand.

"Thank you," said Grainger, matching Martha's neutral expression, although the lawyer's eyes were glittering brightly. "If you don't mind, we have some requests to make before we begin."

Her left hand was resting on the table between the two sides, and as Krisha took a breath to say something she raised her left hand. "I know you'll feel this is putting the cart before the horse, but once you see the video clip, I think you'll understand."

Martha said nothing but raised a sceptical eyebrow, which Grainger ignored. It seemed that she was now at the point she wanted to be.

"What you're about to see will change your perceptions . . . utterly." She clapped her hands together with a sharp smacking noise. "I have worked in this business for nearly thirty years, and I've never seen evidence like this."

Martha frowned slightly as she wondered what the lawyer could be talking about. "If you're asking us to keep an open mind, I can assure you that we both will — and so will all the senior officers on this case. To remind you, the deputy chief constable is closely involved, and he would not tolerate any lack of professionalism."

Now Grainger looked abashed. "I'm sorry. That did sound rather more like a judgement on the quality of your work than I intended. What I'm trying to say is that this evidence — in my opinion — is going to turn this case upside down.

"And for your information, I only received it shortly after you both left the room. It came in an email which has accompanying notes. I will make all of this available to you once we have viewed it together."

"Well, let's find out what you've got and then we can run through some questions," said Martha, "of which, I can assure you, there are going to be a great many." She was determined to get this rolling. Either the lawyer was trying to make fools of everyone, or she really did have something of crucial importance. It was time to find out.

As though she had read her mind, Grainger nodded in agreement.

"Let me get this set up on my iPad and then you'll know what I'm talking about."

CHAPTER 51

"I got something out of the little git," said Harry. "Once I'd explained things to him, he was more than happy to 'help with our inquiries'."

Julie was back in the old routine — making sure Betty was safe while she was at school. She laughed knowingly at the idea of the retired sergeant as an enthusiastic helper. "You were obviously at your most charming."

"I was," said Harry. "Once I stopped slapping him."

"Very droll," said Julie. "I have to admit that if I wasn't back on close protection, I'd have enjoyed coming to meet our friend. From what Martha told us, it would have been interesting to discuss the role of women in the workplace. Anyway, I can tell you're pleased. So, what is it?"

The rasping sound that emerged from her speaker was Harry laughing. Despite being an enthusiastic smoker, Harry had got to seventy-five without any obvious ill effects other than the ability to make some alarming noises. He occasionally produced a cough that seemed to have a life of its own.

"I know that laugh. It means you're up to something."

"Not exactly, but I need to show you something. It can wait until you get home."

"Any clues?" asked Julie. "It's a good job Betty's coming home early at lunchtime today. I'd be fit to burst if I had to wait until this afternoon."

"OK. I can offer you a small clue. You could say it's a sort of vision."

"Visions? You worry me sometimes, Harry. I mean at your age we have to consider that you might go a bit weird."

The rasping sound merged from her phone once again.

"Get yourself back here pronto. I take it the bread you've left on the kitchen table is to make a sandwich for Betty. Shall I do something for all three of us?"

"That you can. This guard duty always make me hungry. I also bought a bag of donuts, they're in the cupboard."

* * *

Harry surveyed the plate of ham-and-tomato sandwiches with the satisfied air of a chef congratulating himself on a job well done. There were a lot of them, probably twice as many as most might do, but most people didn't have to feed Julie, who needed to eat twice as much as everyone else. He checked his watch and calculated that Julie and Betty were minutes away. He decided to go and meet them outside.

Stepping out of the front door he glanced to his left and saw Julie and Betty turning into the road. He made to go out to the pavement but stepped back to allow a jogger to go past. The man's technique was poor, his feet slapping down hard on the pavement and his splayed feet pulling him from side to side. Not for the first time, Harry noted that a lot of joggers were probably doing themselves more harm than good. The man lurched past, and Harry stepped out, waving at Julie and Betty as he did, making the little girl beam as she put on a spurt of speed, her running technique making her glide over the footpath. Seconds later he had scooped her up as the jogger approached Julie.

Harry felt like he'd been enfolded in ice; something was familiar about the jogger. Then he realised he knew him. His mouth opened to shout a warning to Julie, but he was too late. The jogger had drawn level with her and appeared to hit her in the top of the thigh with something he was holding in his left hand. Then he turned into an athlete, sprinting away at top speed, disappearing into the distance.

Grinning maniacally, Julie waved Harry away, flashing a quick thumbs-up to show she was walking wounded. Harry knew she didn't want Betty to realise something had happened. He understood and called out, "Come on, slowcoach, or Betty will eat all your sandwiches." The little girl laughed delightedly at the thought and, wriggling free of Harry, ran inside.

He waited until Julie walked up then made sure Betty was out of earshot. "What happened?"

"He stabbed me," said Julie. "Right in the top of my thigh. I think it's a flesh wound, so I should be able to bandage myself up."

"I feel terrible about this," said Harry. "He ran right past me and was up to you before I put two and two together. He really fooled me."

"So, you recognised him?"

"Yeah, I did. That was 'Marvellous Marcus', aka the 'Diamond Geezer'."

Julie gave him an expectant look.

"He trained as a jeweller and was a very good one by all accounts, but he turned his back on it after discovering he had a talent for crime. He got the nickname 'Diamond Geezer' because he has diamonds embedded in his top teeth."

"What about 'Marvellous Marcus'?"

Harry shrugged. "It's got a good ring to it."

"With all these names I feel like I've been attacked by a gang, not one person. But are you saying he specialises in jewellery?" Julie was looking puzzled.

"He's a bit more than that. He's a stone-cold killer. You just met the most ruthless hitman in Britain. His minimum price is a million pounds with expenses on top. He's made a mint over the years, and I've heard he's taken to picking and choosing his jobs, turning down most assignments regardless of the amount on offer."

"Why's he turned up and attacked me, then? There's nothing special about me, surely? And if he's so shit hot, how come I'm still breathing?"

"That's the million-dollar question, and I think I can guess who's behind it."

"Neil 'Arsehole' Thompson."

Harry nodded, unable to hide the flicker of unease that crossed his face. That look worried Julie. Harry didn't do unease. Not until now.

"We need to be even more careful. Marcus doesn't make mistakes. If he'd wanted you dead . . ." Harry's voice tailed off. "We have to assume that he'll be back, and next time he won't be looking to let us off the hook."

CHAPTER 52

Grainger hit the stop button and sat back in her seat to be met with a stunned silence. Even Imelda had lost her smirk and was staring open-mouthed at the iPad.

"What the fuck did we just watch?" Krisha was the first to break the silence, her words reaching Martha from what seemed like a long way away.

"As you can see, this is a game changer," said Grainger. Martha looked at her closely but could detect no signs of triumph. Even though she had seen the video clip and knew what was coming, the lawyer was still affected by it.

"I think we need to see that again. I suspect we may need to see it several times."

Grainger nodded and went to hit the play button, but Imelda whispered something to her lawyer, who nodded and looked at Martha. "My client would appreciate a toilet break."

Martha was already standing up. "I'll leave you with the custody officer and we can start again in say fifteen minutes. Do say if you need food or a drink."

With no objection from Grainger, she tapped Krisha on the shoulder and the two women quickly walked out of the room.

"We're going to need people smarter than us watching that clip," said Martha. Her adrenaline up, she made a conscious effort to breathe slowly and deeply. "I think we go through it again then step out and organise all the people we are going to need. And if I'm honest I'm not entirely sure who that should be."

"I've got a few thoughts on that," said Krisha. "The lawyer mentioned something about 'neurological conditioning', so we need a neurologist. My dad's got dementia and we've been talking to a lovely neurologist. He's been a real help."

"I'm sorry to hear that about your dad," Martha said, her eyes widening slightly in sympathy.

"Once we've got this done, I'll tell you all about it," said Krisha. "But you agree with the idea?"

"I do. I also think we have no choice but to get GCHQ involved. They're the best people to analyse the video clip. The sooner we can get the clip to them the better. I want to know if it's real. Is what we've seen actually possible or is it some sort of deep fake?" She looked up towards the ceiling. "This is probably naïve, but knowing who sent it would be good."

"That may sound like a daft question to a techie, but as a police officer that's what we need to know," Krisha agreed as she chewed delicately at a fingernail. "Basically, you want anything and everything. And you'd probably like it by yesterday?"

"That's about the size of it. But what do you make it of so far?"

"I don't quite know what to think," said Krisha, looking perplexed. "I think we can agree with the lawyer that this is like nothing else any of us has ever seen. It's like those Matt Damon movies."

"You're right, the Jason Bourne films. I do hope there's no real similarity. I don't want to discover we've blundered into something top secret."

"It's possible," said Krisha. "But I don't think our own government is behind this. They wouldn't be going around murdering innocent people." She spoke with a conviction that was only slightly undermined by her doubtful expression.

"Let's keep an open mind and keep talking. I'm baffled by this and it's easy to get sucked into thinking like a conspiracy clown. Especially when you suspect that we're in the middle of a huge conspiracy that's somehow aimed at me." She reached her arms over her head and stretched.

"Let's go back inside and try to make some sense out of this. I have a horrible feeling we're going to struggle to find the right crime to charge Imelda with. I mean, I know she did it, you know it, her lawyer knows it and she knows it. So, how can they be claiming it wasn't her? The answer has to be inside that room."

CHAPTER 53

Julie walked into the kitchen, where Betty was enthusiastically eating a pink-coated donut while regaling Harry about her morning at school. In response to his raised eyebrow, she patted her leg lightly.

"Just a bit of gauze and some tape," she reassured him. She could tell he was still concerned about the confrontation with Marcus.

"Are you OK to watch over Betty? I've got a few phone calls to make." He gave her a meaningful look, and she knew he was going to get his contacts out asking questions.

"Do you think it might have something to do with your trip this morning?"

"Maybe," said Harry, looking doubtful. "But it would be pretty quick of them. I know for a fact that Marcus never does anything without a lot of planning. And I couldn't have made it clearer to our friend that he was to keep quiet."

"Are we going to see one of your friends, Harry?" asked Betty, who had now finished off her donut.

"Not today, sweetie," said Harry. "And what have I always said about small people with big ears?"

"That we hear everything," announced the triumphant little girl.

"You do. Now, can you be a good girl while Julie has her lunch and then maybe we'll all go to the park?"

"OK." The little girl looked solemnly at Julie. "Harry says you can eat more than anyone he knows."

"Like I said: small person, big ears." He beat a hasty retreat. Julie watched him head out of the front door then opened the fridge, rubbing her hands together when she saw her share of sandwiches. She didn't care who knew about her eating habits.

Halfway through her meal she remembered that Harry was supposed to have shown her something. Something he'd seemed very interested in a few hours ago. Carefully brushing some crumbs off her T-shirt, she knew that with all the excitement going on she would have to wait to find out what it was he'd collected in Surrey.

About half an hour later, her phone beeped with a message from Harry: *I'll see you in the park in a few minutes. I've checked around and all is quiet right now. I'll fill you in properly once you get here.*

Why all the mystery? Julie wondered. She sighed. The best thing she could do now was focus on Betty.

"Are you ready for the park yet, young lady?"

"I was born ready," she said, to Julie's amusement.

"Where did you hear that?"

"It was in the new *Leo the Lion* film."

"Well, if you're sure you're ready, we might as well go." As they left the house, Julie looked carefully around. She had suddenly developed a distrust of stray joggers.

They got to the swings to find Harry already there. He reached inside his jacket pocket, coming out with what she thought looked like a photograph.

"Have a look at this."

CHAPTER 54

This time there was no interruption as Grainger hit the play button. The clip was compelling — if unnerving — viewing, and this time Martha tried to be as analytical as possible as she watched again. The film began with Imelda walking into a bedroom and sitting on the edge of an unmade bed. She was wearing a T-shirt and jeans that were rumpled enough to suggest they'd been worn for a couple of days. From the light coming in through the window, it appeared to be daytime, but it was impossible to say exactly what the time was, although Martha had the sense it was early morning. There was no audio and the date and timestamp were missing.

Imelda looked up and spoke to someone out of view, then she held her left arm out and away from her body. Someone, it was impossible to see who, came into the edge of the shot. Then the camera angle changed. Before it had been face on to Imelda, now it shifted through ninety degrees so it gave a clear, side-on shot. The unknown person had grabbed Imelda's arm and was tapping on the veins where the limb was jointed. Then a hypodermic needle was inserted, and the contents injected. Imelda showed no response to this, and that portion of the film ended with a close-up on a medical label which read, SCOPOLAMINE.

"Stop it there, please." Martha's voice sounded loud in the quiet of the interview room. She steepled her fingers in front of her. "Was this taken in your bedroom, Imelda?"

It was the first direct question she'd asked their prime suspect in a while. Like before it was greeted with a slight shrug, but this time Imelda leaned over to Grainger and whispered in her ear.

"My client says she can't be certain it is her bedroom, although she thinks it is." Grainger's expression gave nothing away.

"Can you recall what the film shows — that is, you being injected?" Again, she directed the question at Imelda and again her suspect refused to make eye contact, but leaned across to the lawyer. This time there was a longer exchange between the pair.

"My client says she has no recollection of this event or anything like it. She does confirm that it is her on film, however, and says the first time she saw this was in this interview room."

"What about the person who injected you?"

More whispering.

"She has no idea. She does not recognise the person."

"This film suggests you were injected with a drug called scopolamine. Is this a drug you're familiar with? It has a reputation for making people vulnerable to mind control. From what I've read, it lowers people's natural resistance to committing crimes and leaving victims with no recollection of what they've done."

As she finished, Krisha was looking at her speculatively, so Martha continued, "It was on that course I mentioned, the one about mind-control techniques. He claimed scopolamine was used by criminals in South America by drugging victims' drinks in bars. Apparently, it reduces inhibitions. People claim to have been taken to cash machines to empty their bank accounts but have no recollection of it happening. It's known as Devil's Breath."

Suddenly Imelda surprised everyone, including her lawyer, by speaking.

"I don't do drugs." She spoke with a strong London accent.

"Well, the clip suggests someone was injecting you with a drug. Are you aware of scopolamine's reputation?" Martha kept her tone reasonable, desperate to try and build some form of relationship with Imelda.

"I told you. I don't do drugs." Imelda's eyes were blazing, and Grainger interjected.

"My client is making it clear that she would not voluntarily take drugs and she has no idea what scopolamine does. All she knows is what I told you the first time we saw this and which you have repeated, that scopolamine has a reputation for use as a mind-control drug. There is plenty of evidence which says people given this drug lose both their inhibitions and memory."

Martha thought about the answer and decided to return to it. She checked Krisha had no questions and then asked Grainger to repeat the clip.

"Imelda, I need to keep asking you questions. Do you understand?"

"I get it, of course I do. I'm not stupid."

"No one is suggesting you are," said Martha, who couldn't quite hide her surprise at getting such a positive response. "As I say, I need to ask you questions. So, as before: do you know where this was shot?"

"No."

"Do you remember anything about this?"

"No."

"Did you kill anyone after watching this?"

"I don't know." A look flashed across her face which might have been uncertainty, so Martha pushed harder.

"Are you sure about that?"

"I'm telling you the truth when I say I can't remember, but when I try my brain goes all sort of fuzzy. Like someone has scrubbed that bit of memory."

"And there's nothing there at all?"

"No, I told you." Beads of sweat appeared on her brow and Grainger intervened. "We could do with five minutes, please. My client is understandably stressed at repeatedly having to watch evidence which clearly shows she has been manipulated and violated."

Martha and Krisha stepped outside.

"What do you think?"

"Honest answer?" Krisha grimaced. She checked no one was in hearing range. "There's something going on here. The question to me is how much she wanted to do this and how much is down to persuasion by a third party."

"I agree with you," said Martha leaning against the wall. "I still think she's a psychopath, but I suppose even psychopaths can get played. It seems plain to me that this video is intended to show she was under the control of someone else when she committed the crime, effectively making her the weapon rather than the killer."

"So, what do we do now? Kick it upstairs with a note saying, 'Here's a murderer, we know she did it but someone else made her do it'? What would you do?"

"It may come to that but first let's get those expert opinions we've been talking about. I'd like to know how plausible it is for this drug to allow people to control others. And since we both think this might be mind control, it's definitely one for GCHQ." She waggled her eyebrows. "From what I've heard, the spooks are always dabbling in this sort of thing. They must know a thing or two by now."

CHAPTER 55

The grainy photograph showed a man in his forties or fifties walking through Covent Garden. He was looking straight ahead, and it almost appeared as if he knew he was being snapped. His features were obscured by a trilby hat pulled down low, so it was hard to get a clear impression of him, especially as he had the collar of his coat pulled up.

"Is this him? Is this Neil Thompson?" Julie's expression had frozen in a grimace. "God, I'd like to strangle the bastard." Her fingers curled round the edges of the print, making Harry hurriedly reach out and gently touch her hand.

"That's the only copy I've got."

"Why haven't you got it on your phone?"

"I prefer bits of paper," Harry replied with a shrug.

"You don't know how to do it, do you?"

"Never mind about that," said Harry. "You can sort it out for me. I mean why have a dog and bark yourself?"

Julie rolled her eyes but said nothing. Instead, she pulled out her phone and photographed the photograph. Once she was happy she had it, she threw a questioning look Harry's way.

"It was taken six months ago by Edwards, and he says Neil Thompson doesn't know it exists. He says it was sheer chance he got it because it was the only time that he ever met Thompson."

"How did that creep do something that everyone else has failed to do?" asked Julie.

"I asked him exactly that, and I'm inclined to believe him as I had my foot pressed right into his groin at the time. He says that he was taking some general pictures to show his wife of the area."

"Why?" demanded Julie.

"He said his wife used to love Covent Garden, they hadn't been up there for years, and he wanted to show her how it looked today. When he got home, he was surprised to find an image of our man in among the tourist shots."

"OK . . ." Julie managed to inject a world of doubt into a tiny word. "Let's run with this unlikely story for a while. How does he know it's Neil Thompson?"

"He says everyone at the meeting called him by that name. And I hope you don't think I'm getting soft in my old age; I did give the sergeant the impression he would be singing soprano if he messed me around."

"You're the last person I'd doubt. I'm playing devil's advocate. You mentioned a meeting."

"Yes, he claims they were summoned to an emergency meeting, him and three others he didn't know, then Thompson turned up and shut it all down without an explanation."

"And why hold it in the middle of a tourist area?"

"I asked that as well and he has no idea."

"So, a bit of a mystery. OK, we go along with this for now, with a few doubts on the side?"

Harry nodded his assent, so Julie had another long look at the picture.

"He doesn't look like a criminal mastermind." She stared some more. "In fact, if you walked past him in the street you wouldn't look twice. If anything, he looks like one of those boring relatives you try to avoid sitting next to at family get-togethers."

She held the picture out at arm's length, trying through sheer willpower to pick up some psychic clues about what the man was like. Her eyes bored into the picture.

Harry broke her concentration. "You're pulling a very odd face. Do you need the loo?"

She gave him a mock-fierce expression. "I was just thinking you can't judge by appearances. He looks harmless in this picture. At last, we have a picture of our enemy. I know you can't see much, but at least it's a start."

"Something we've needed for a while," said Harry. "I'm looking forward to seeing what Martha makes of it. It feels like we're making some progress after a long run of no luck whatsoever."

"What about Martha's idea of using Edwards to contact Thompson? Any progress on that?"

"You know I don't like that idea at all," said Harry. Now it was his turn to look fierce. "I'm hoping this picture will make her feel more positive that we can beat this man without having to grovel to him. Her dad always said, 'Harry — first know your enemy' and, if this is him, we're making progress on that front."

"Have you told Martha about it yet?"

An emphatic shake of the head. "You know I don't trust mobiles, too many people listening in. And there's no way I'm ringing a police switchboard and asking to be put through. I sent a text a few hours ago to say I had something she'd be interested in, but she hasn't got back to me, which is odd. She normally calls back pretty quickly."

CHAPTER 56

Martha walked back into the interview room and instantly sensed there had been a change for the worse, even though at first glance nothing had altered. Imelda and Grainger were as she had left them minutes ago, calm and quiet with their hands folded in their laps. The uniformed PC was still standing in exactly the same spot and no one else had entered. Yet it felt profoundly different, as though the atmosphere had become more threatening, sending chills racing up her spine. She turned to see if anyone had followed her in, but only Krisha was standing there, giving her a small smile of encouragement.

Sitting down, she looked directly at Imelda and recoiled as she took in the unnatural glitter of her eyes. Then her conscious brain took in what her subconscious had been shouting at her. Imelda's pupils were enormous, dominating the visible part of her eyes like miniature black holes. Martha sensed that some sort of fundamental change had taken place. But what? Part of her wondered if some sort of trigger word had tipped her over the edge but before she could explore the idea, Imelda smiled. It wasn't a warm smile; it was imbued with an unnerving mix of malice and triumph. Martha went to speak, trying to get back on the front foot, but her mouth was dry and her lips stuck together. She was reaching for some water when Imelda spoke.

"I have something to say. Well, actually, Neil has something to say. He'd love to be here himself to tell you in person, but you'll have to put up with me." She stopped and looked at Martha with a fierce intensity that was almost physical. The pause lasted almost five seconds but seemed longer. Then Imelda spoke again.

"Neil asked me to keep this simple, so you'd understand. The big takeaway for you is that I'm doing everything by my own choice. Not in a way you'd understand, but this is about me and Neil agreeing a way forward." She leaned a little closer and that smirk reappeared. "He told me I have the perfect mind to do this."

Then she stopped again and looked at Martha once more. Her eyes were wet, and she looked feverish. Imelda started to move, and Martha, every instinct on high alert, reacted fast, reaching across the table to try and restrain her, but fast as she was, it was too late.

Imelda, now grinning maniacally, reached across to where Grainger was sitting, plucked the ball point pen from the solicitor's fingers and smashed it into her own left eye. For the briefest moment she sat there, presenting a grotesque picture as blood and jelly-like fluid started to pour from her ruined eye down over her nose and mouth. Then, without a sound and still grinning, she slammed her face down on the table, the pen disappearing into her brain with a sickening crunching sound.

As Imelda lay there, her body twitching in its death throes, Martha felt she had woken to a living nightmare. Beside her Krisha was screaming "No!" and had knocked her chair over as she leaped up in shock. The young policeman was puking into the corner and Grainger had fallen off her chair in a dead faint, her bladder having given way. Martha couldn't help but look down to see if she had done the same thing and was relieved to find she hadn't. Still feeling like she was in a nightmare, she hit the panic button although there was little anyone would be able to do.

Neil Thompson had sent her a clear message. *No, not a message*, she reminded herself — it was a threat. *See what I can make people do if I get the chance. Maybe the next one will be someone you love.*

She should have been terrified, but he'd made a big mistake. He'd totally underestimated who he was dealing with. Not just Martha herself, but all of her friends, who were as tough as they came. She felt a sense of pity for Imelda. She was clearly so damaged she was vulnerable to manipulation. Her body filled with cold rage. If she'd hated the man before, now she loathed him with every fibre of her being. That was the moment she stopped being the hunted and became the hunter.

CHAPTER 57

"If necessary, can you take charge in here, at least for the time being? The investigation team are going to want details," said Martha.

"Your family and friends come first," said Krisha, leaning forward to gently squeeze Martha's hands. "Go and do what you need to do. I'll talk to the chief inspector, make sure he knows what's going on. There's no doubt in my mind that he wants you to think that he can get at people close to you and control them the way he controlled Imelda. As long as this man is free, you and your family are in danger. You have to deal with that first."

Martha could sense the intensity behind her words. Not for the first time she was grateful for Krisha's empathy and sharp intelligence. She hadn't needed to explain herself, and felt that she'd left a complex and desperately unpleasant situation in safe hands. She set off, forcing herself not to run, and was soon out of the building, stepping away from the busy high street to find a quiet spot where she could call Harry.

* * *

"You must be psychic. We were just thinking about you. We've made a breakthrough in—"

"Harry. Stop. There's something vital I have to tell you," said Martha.

"OK, I'm listening," Harry replied, instantly alert.

"Julie needs to listen in as well. Is it alright to put me on speaker?"

He glanced around the play area, checking that no one was near enough to overhear, and at the same time beckoned Julie closer, pointing at the phone. "You can talk now, Martha, we're both listening."

"We're all in terrible danger. Neil Thompson's worked out some way of controlling people to do anything he wants. I've just seen Imelda Taylor kill herself in the most horrific way and he got her to do it simply as a message to me."

"How is that even possible?" said Julie.

"I wish I knew. It's got something to do with a drug called scopolamine and he's using TikTok to send instructions which victims are powerless to resist." Martha was speaking too fast, which Harry knew was down to stress. Looking around again he noted there was still no one in earshot and Betty was playing happily on the swing. Then it hit him. Martha's daughter could be a target.

"Let's put worrying about how he did it to one side," said Harry. "I'll take your word he can do it. So, priorities? Shall we deal with Betty first?"

"You took the words out of my mouth." Martha didn't try to hide the note of gratitude that crept into her voice. "Unless either of you has a better idea, I was wondering if there was somewhere Betty could hide away in safety?"

The two shared a glance and Harry shook his head. "The only places I can think of aren't really suitable for a child. What about you, Julie?"

"I know a place that will work, it's at my—"

"Don't say it out loud and don't even tell me, at least not the details," Martha hissed. "Her safety is going to depend on secrecy. If I'm grabbed, then at least I can't give away her address."

"I can help with that," said Harry, sounding even brisker than before as the scale of the threat they were facing continued to sink in. "Let me make a few phone calls then I can sort out the transport and beef up security. I'll run everything by you, but a few more 'faces' around the place can't hurt. Are you coming straight back here?"

"I was on my way, but talking to you guys, I wonder if I might get in the way of the plan. Maybe I need to stick around here for a little while, help the investigation team get going. Although I doubt anyone will be able to make sense of it."

There was a prolonged pause, and both Harry and Julie could sense the wrestling match that was going on inside Martha's head. Eventually she started talking again, but now her voice sounded tired. "If everything comes together at your end you may need to get Betty moving before I can get there. You're going to have to go, Julie. I don't like it but it's the only answer I can think of. If I disappear from here then questions will get asked, and that's the last thing we need. Call if you can, but I know I can trust you two to get it right. Can you tell us, in general terms, what you're thinking of doing, Julie?"

"Yeah. And I can keep it general, no clues. I've got a very old mate who lives outside London. We haven't spoken in a while, so there's nothing to connect us, no phone calls, emails or texts. She wrote to me in prison — a real letter — and said if I ever needed help then just to turn up. She's hard as nails and nice as pie. She'll be like a tigress with her cubs when we turn up and explain what's going on."

"Harry, I don't know about you, but that sounds perfect," said Martha, the relief evident in her voice.

"Couldn't agree more," said Harry. "That's exactly the sort of safe house we need. A long way from here and no one knows about it."

"Alright then," said Martha. "I think we've obviously got enough to be going on. Anyone got anything else before I have to get back?"

"Yes, a couple. Along with a car for Julie, I could arrange some security for the journey. Maybe not to follow her all the way but at least out past the M25."

"Good plan," Martha and Julie choroused.

"I'll sort it. Just don't ask me too many questions, especially about the car. The other thing is, that thing I was going to tell you when you rang up. We've got a picture of 'you know who' . . . At least, your friend Sergeant Edwards says it's him, so be careful until we can get it totally confirmed. Julie's got it on her phone so we can ping it to you. I think your need to see it now outstrips our usual worries about security."

"Wow, that's amazing news! I'll look forward to hearing more about how you got it once all of this is behind us."

As the call ended her phone pinged with the arrival of the photograph. Opening the image, she was taken aback by how insignificant the man looked. He was one of those people who could come and go and never be noticed. She shivered. There was something about the way the most twisted individuals could look so innocent, as if butter wouldn't melt in their mouths.

She stared at the photo a little longer trying to see if there was some clue there, something that would give her an edge, but nothing would come. She went to close it down and paused. There was something, she was sure, but the thought remained frustratingly elusive no matter how hard she tried. With an angry shake of her head, she headed back to find Krisha. They had planning to do.

CHAPTER 58

"Is that him? He's the monster?" Krisha was incredulous, then shrugged exaggeratedly. "They all look the same behind bars — we need to nick him."

"It may be him, only maybe. And it's not the best picture I've seen," said Martha. "But I do appreciate your optimism. As soon as this bit is out of the way we can crack on."

"That's fine by me," said Krisha. "There's something at the back of my mind. Hopefully it will come to me while this nonsense gets sorted." She waved her hand vaguely towards the corridor while managing to look even more harassed than before.

"This investigation is a pain," said Martha. "But the Met won't take any chances and likes to be seen to be doing the right thing. Even when they have everything on video and backed up with sound recordings."

"I suppose with your dad being who he was you have good insight."

"I think things were rather looser in his day," said Martha, looking down at the floor. "But that was then, and this is now." She shifted around in her seat, which seemed designed to be as uncomfortable as possible. Even though they had only been sitting there a few minutes her backside was already going numb. The two women were waiting outside an office commandeered by Superintendent Susan Scales, head of the Met's Anti-Corruption Command. Her team had been ordered to investigate Imelda's death to see if there was any suggestion it had been caused by malpractice on behalf of the police, namely Martha as the ranking officer present, even if it was only as acting inspector.

After a few minutes, they were called in to where the superintendent was waiting, standing in front of the desk. She looked, Martha thought, like she'd had bad news. She stared at Martha for a moment before breaking the silence. "Please, call me Susan." She indicated that they sit down.

They nodded their thanks and settled into the two chairs placed in front of the desk. Susan, now sitting again, surveyed them over her spotless desk. Nothing marred the empty space.

"That'll look a bit different in a couple of days," said Susan. "Nothing like an internal investigation to generate paperwork." Her rueful expression spoke volumes for her opinion of red tape.

She looked up. "I don't normally do this but I'm going to say right away that you two are out of the woods. You'll need to be interviewed, but from viewing the video and speaking to the victim's solicitor it's clear you did nothing wrong and did not provoke this tragic incident."

She stopped and smiled at each in turn, then held her hand up, palm outwards. "Silence. Complete and utter silence. I think that will be the best policy from here on in." Susan's mouth had settled in a thin line. "We all know that our best bet of getting anywhere is to keep this out of the public domain as long as possible, because I think we all know what will happen if the media get hold of this, especially that video clip. It's the most disturbing thing I've ever seen. I do have one immediate question though. Who is this Neil Thompson and what is his connection to you, Martha?"

Martha swallowed. Faced with the need to respond immediately she made a snap decision not to mention the photograph. She hoped it wouldn't come back to haunt her.

"I'm not sure who he is, not exactly, but I believe he is a significant figure in organised crime. Why he became involved in this case I don't know, but his links with me go back to when my father did the same job as you. For some reason Thompson tried to have me framed for my mother's murder — very nearly succeeded. I think, and this is a guess, he believes my father was in possession of some information which Thompson didn't want known and believes I may have."

Susan was looking exceptionally sphinx-like, and Martha guessed she knew more than she was letting on.

"And you say the first you knew of Thompson's involvement was when Imelda announced she knew him?"

"That's right," said Martha, hoping her face didn't show her discomfort. "It gave me quite a shock, but I wanted to pursue the interview and see what other information Imelda came up with."

"And you knew nothing about this, Krisha?" Susan's sudden switch almost caught Martha by surprise.

"I was as puzzled as anyone," said Krisha.

Susan let a silence build. It was the classic tactic of inviting them to fill the gap in conversation, but neither of the junior officers fell for it.

Susan sat back. "That will do for now. Don't forget, keep quiet about this as long as possible and don't tell your partner. This case just got a lot more awkward, so tread very carefully. Your Mr Thompson sounds a very dangerous man."

They both nodded their heads earnestly and Susan indicated the door.

Outside Martha thanked Krisha for keeping quiet about the picture. "Did you notice her calling him 'my' Mr Thompson?" she added. "We'll need to be careful around her, she's not quite as friendly as she'd like us to think."

Krisha frowned. "Do you think she might have something to do with Thompson?"

"That's a good question," said Martha, wrapping her arms protectively around herself. "It's so easy to get paranoid, but that may be no bad thing if it keeps us on our toes."

"We'll have to be ultra-careful then," said Krisha, glancing at her friend. "I'm always here for you if you need anything."

Martha, who was desperate to get home before Betty left, smiled at Krisha. "Thank you for that. You're turning into a good friend."

Krisha looked awkward and Martha patted her arm. "See you again very soon."

CHAPTER 59

"I don't know about you, but they scare me." Julie was only partly joking as she surveyed the group of men and women that Harry had assembled in super-quick time. Two of the men were significantly bigger than Julie, who was a giant by anyone's standards, and all gave off an air of menace that suggested it would be deeply unwise to get in a fight with any of them. But perhaps the scariest one — in a group of truly scary people — was the young woman, who somehow managed to find a pocket of space in what was the seriously overcrowded kitchen at Martha's house. Julie couldn't put her finger on why she was so scary — she wasn't especially big or muscley, but she looked terrifyingly efficient, like crossing her would see you sliced and diced as if you'd fallen into an industrial mixer.

"I see you've noticed Antoinette, or Frenchie to her friends," said Harry. "I was going to suggest she drives you where you're going and brings the car back. There's no one better at close protection, and although she doesn't say much, she does have a very good rapport with kids, so she'll help keep Betty's spirits up. You might even want her to stay with you, but that's obviously down to you and your friend."

All the time he was talking, 'Scary Toni', as Julie was starting to think of her, stared at her, never once appearing to blink. Harry was moving on. "These four—" he indicated a group of biggish men with an assortment of scars and all with poorly reset broken noses — "will be following you split between two cars. And I know amateurs like to say having scars is a sign of a poor operator — well, these guys have a lot of scars because they have a lot of fights."

The remark punctured a tense atmosphere which was in danger of making everyone nervous. One of the two really gigantic men grinned at Julie.

"All the others," said Harry, waving an arm to take in the rest of the people in the kitchen, "will be part of the new security details here, but for now you won't need to worry about that. As with Frenchie, if you want any of these four to stay with you just ask. Or I can send more people to you."

As she looked around, Julie felt oddly moved at being with the group Harry had assembled at such short notice.

"I take it you've told everyone about what a nasty piece of work we're up against?"

"For sure," said Harry. With a jolt of surprise, she noticed that Scary Toni had produced a lethal-looking stiletto from somewhere and was using it to clean her fingernails. Even the really big guys edged a little further away.

"Everyone is fully tooled up and will do what is necessary. Talking of which, I have a few little toys for you."

He picked up an old-fashioned Gladstone bag and handed it to her. It felt gratifyingly heavy.

"Everything you'll need, plus ammo. Have a look, and if there's anything you want to change let me know."

Having got their instructions from Harry, everyone filed out silently.

"That lot are the best of the best. Everyone has ties to me, even a few to Martha, and know what they're up against. They're getting well paid, but they're also volunteers — at least in a way. They joined up despite knowing the nature of what they're going to face, so you can rely on them with your life."

"You can't have arranged this with a couple of phone calls?" asked Julie.

"Not even close," said Harry, who was looking as sombre as she'd ever seen him. "I've been worried about the way things were going for a while. I didn't want to alarm Martha, so I kept it to myself. I was determined not to get caught out for want of effort."

"Maybe I should keep your people with me," said a thoughtful-looking Julie. "My friend lives in a huge place so there'll be plenty of room for everyone."

"I've spoken to everyone individually, so they all know what's at stake," responded Harry. "From this moment they answer to you and no one else."

Once again Julie was caught up in emotion, and she began to well up.

"In less than an hour I'll be on my way with Betty and leaving you guys behind. Just keep everyone safe for me."

Running out of words, she embraced Harry in a bear hug, which he responded to with a hug of his own.

"We're ready for anything," said Harry, holding her by the shoulders. "But you have the biggest job of all, keeping Betty safe. How's she taking it?"

"She's brilliant as always," said Julie. "We've spoken to Martha — I think she'll be back by the time we're ready to go on our 'long holiday in the countryside'."

Their conversation was interrupted by the return of Frenchie. "I promised Betty I'd iron this Paddington Bear T-shirt. Can you point me in the right direction?" She spoke in a surprisingly gentle voice.

"I didn't have you down as the domestic type," said Julie.

"Only for people I like," came the reply.

An hour later, the convoy of three cars headed away from Martha's home in Dulwich. Martha just made it home in time to hug her daughter, fighting back tears as she held her in her arms. Finally putting her down, she watched proudly as the little girl solemnly fist-bumped with her security detail. Martha kept the biggest, brightest smile pasted on her face, but Harry looked away. With so much at stake, even the great man was feeling the tension. If he hadn't got this right, he wasn't sure he'd be able to live with the consequences.

CHAPTER 60

Martha felt bone-weary, and parting from her daughter took most of her reserves, but she managed to drag herself back to her 'day job', where Krisha's enthusiasm was restoring her own drive.

"Jonathan Roper . . . Does the name ring a bell?" Krisha was looking earnestly at her friend, who'd returned from waving her daughter off looking like she had the weight of the world on her shoulders.

It took a moment but the mildly baffled look on Martha's face was replaced with a brighter expression. "He's the guy who works with DCI Brian Hooley? Both said to be very smart detectives, if I'm thinking of the right men?"

"That's them. The DCI says Roper's the most talented investigator he's ever worked with, a real brainbox, and that's saying something. Hooley's a bit of a legend, worked with some of the best."

"Sounds good so far," said Martha. "Tell me why I should be interested in Roper."

"I've remembered something about him which may help." The way she chewed at her bottom lip betrayed she was feeling less than certain.

Martha was intrigued but said nothing, giving her friend a little space to work in.

"I was told that Roper's a brilliant analyst. Apparently, he's autistic, and in his case it means he has a tremendous ability to concentrate and memorise things. Much more than most people. At least that's what I heard."

"I don't know a lot about autism, I must admit," said Martha. "I was told it's a spectrum condition with people at all different points and different abilities. I'm not sure how this helps us though."

"Sorry, I'm rambling a bit," said Krisha. "The point is he's so good at data analysis he often gets seconded to GCHQ stuff, helping out there. He's not a policeman as such, but his skills make him an ace detective. I was told that if you can grab his attention, he can help by using his access to resources we can only guess at."

"And that could include facial recognition and background material we wouldn't get to see normally." Martha was smiling. "Well done, Krisha, this might be the break we're looking for. Do you want to set up a meeting with him? We badly need that break."

* * *

It took Krisha longer to find Roper's number than it did to talk to him. She outlined the case and explained why they needed his help, then listened intently as he asked a series of questions. Minutes later, she thanked him profusely and put the phone down.

"He said to come round now. His boss is away on a conference, so he has the office to himself."

Martha set a brisk pace for the exit, and as they headed for the tube station they passed a bakery, enticing smells wafting out into the air.

"Tell you what," said Krisha. "Do you fancy getting something to eat, even if it's just a sausage roll? I need to get half a dozen chocolate donuts for Roper."

"Six donuts?" said Martha incredulously. "I thought cops stuffing themselves with donuts was a myth. Our bloke must be the size of a house."

Forty-five minutes later, Martha was re-evaluating that opinion as she shook hands with the lanky investigator, who didn't appear to have an ounce of fat on him. He had an upright appearance made more so by the expensive-looking but slightly out-of-date black suit he was wearing. He was polite and formal, if a little reserved, but she noted his eyes looking at her inquisitively.

"I've heard of your father," he announced, taking her by surprise. "An interesting man. I shouldn't be at all surprised if your request somehow reaches back to your dad."

Both Krisha and Martha stared at him. "How could you know that?"

"Just a bit of detective work and some advanced analytics," he replied enigmatically. He rubbed his hands together. "I see you have donuts. I'm starving. Would you care to join me?"

In the space it took them to decline, he'd eaten his first one, swiftly followed by two more, before carefully washing his hands with a moist tissue.

"That's better. Let's get to work. I believe you have a picture to show me. First things first, send it to the number I've texted you." Martha's phone pinged even though he hadn't appeared to do anything. She managed to bite down on her surprise. They were clearly in the presence of someone who knew their way around technology, certainly better than she could.

"Whose number is that?" asked Krisha, determined not to show she was intimidated by Roper's obvious skills.

"Oh, just someone who can access a rather sophisticated facial recognition system. It will start with UK and US databases. Hopefully what we need will come up."

"And no one minds you dipping into this stuff?" asked Martha. "I thought this was all top secret."

"It's true you need the right access, but I do a lot of work for the people who created the system. In return, they know they can trust me, and I gain access when I need it. Like now. If I messed about, I'd lose access immediately."

"How long will it take and how much can you trust the information?" said Martha.

"I read in the files that your father was a direct man and very careful, liked to think ahead. I see you're much the same. If Brian was here, he'd say 'like father, like daughter'. I expect he worked for your dad." He looked at Martha with that peculiarly direct gaze. "But to answer your questions: first, it takes as long as it takes; second, you can trust the information if it comes from a trustworthy source . . . remember you're taking someone else's word for it."

Martha tilted her head to one side. Jonathan was one of the most interesting detectives she had ever met, and she marvelled at his bright and inquiring mind. She guessed that once you got to know him, he would make a great colleague, even a loyal friend. She had the sense he was a man who valued the truth above all else. While she had never previously known anything about him, she could sense he was a man who, like his boss, Brian Hooley, would prove to be a tough, no-nonsense man with a reputation for not taking prisoners.

All three checked their emails while waiting, hoping to get a quick result, and a few minutes later Jonathan's phone pinged. Martha's heart was in her mouth as she watched him opening a message. He read it quickly then looked up. "How interesting."

CHAPTER 61

"He's a what!" said Harry. Not much made him shout out loud like this.

"Neil Thompson, or perhaps I should say, the man in the photograph you extracted from Roger Edwards, makes his living out of selling information — the sort of information you don't find with an internet search. Sometimes he does things for intelligence agencies, including our own MI5." Martha repeated each word carefully to ensure there was no possibility of being misheard. Krisha, who was watching closely, recognised the peculiar expression that had appeared on his face — it one she had herself been sporting since Jonathan Roper had talked them through the results of his searches through top-secret databases. He'd made them hold their hands up and swear they would never reveal where they'd got the information from. "It is a matter of National Security," he'd said quite sincerely.

"But how do you know you can trust us?" asked Martha. "You've only just met us."

"My boss is aware of you both and only has good things to say about you." She was so surprised her mouth had dropped open. She went to ask another question then decided against it. He was helping them, so why push it any further?

After their vow of secrecy, he'd forwarded them the information. "Some of the material about him is redacted, but there's still plenty here. Including some addresses where he is known to operate from.

"Neil Thompson is an alias he's known to use. We don't know what his real name is. Up to today they only ever had one picture of him, and he's notoriously careful about covering his tracks. I've requested access to the picture the intelligence services have, but there's an argument that allowing you to see it would compromise very sensitive, classified information."

As an exasperated look flicked across their faces it brought a fleeting smile to his. "That world is not for everyone. But I'm hopeful we'll get something, maybe a headshot."

Now they were back at Idmiston Road and feeding the information to an incredulous Harry. Martha had sent him a text, but he announced he preferred a verbal brief, which she was providing.

"As we feared, the man we're calling Neil Thompson is a very serious player in the crime world. He boasts formidable contacts and is said to oversee a significant operation which gives him access to highly trained mercenaries and killers. He also values secrecy above everything, and his people face death if they break the code of silence. Roper was incredibly impressed you'd got something from Edwards, and I quote, 'Your Harry must be scary indeed if he's more frightening than Neil Thompson.'

"We thought we were up against a top criminal, but in a way he's more than that. It's like he's some sort of crime broker — a crime lord, even." She gasped. "I'm parched, all this excitement is getting to me."

Harry made no comment, and she realised he was lost in memories. After a few moments he said, "A long time ago, thirty years or more, there was talk that your dad had a contact who could get their hands on information about anything. I say thirty years ago, make it more like forty . . ." He trailed off. After a moment or two he shook his head.

"I was wondering if they could be one and the same, but I don't see how. The man in our picture is about fifty, so he'd have been about ten years old to be the same man your dad spoke to. The only reason I wondered if they were linked was because this man could even find out MI5's secrets. I suppose these types, these 'brokers' as you call them, Martha, are much the same."

Martha gulped down a glass of water then handed one to Krisha. "I think my brain is going to overload any minute." She sat down at the kitchen table and rubbed her eyes, then sat up straight, the characteristic gleam reappearing in her eyes. "The question is, what can we do?"

Harry looked puzzled. "When?"

"In the next forty-eight hours," said Martha. "Roper's going to tell his boss what we have so far, at which point all sorts of people get involved, including spies. You can bet they'll be all over the Bankside flat where Imelda was picked up."

"Then there's no time to waste."

"What did you have in mind?" asked Martha, looking closely at Harry.

"Roper's information might prove golden or lead us up a dead end, but if time is ticking, there's no sense in hanging back. This could be the opportunity I've been waiting for. I've got a couple of blokes, ex-special forces, who know what they're doing. If they find our friend, then . . . they know what to do."

"Come on, Harry, what does that mean?"

Harry's head went down for a moment, but then he looked up and made eye contact with her.

"They kill him. No questions. No waiting for approval. Just shoot him in the face."

CHAPTER 62

Martha tried her best to persuade Harry that there was another option — but he wasn't in the mood to listen.

"I've got one job, and that's protecting you and Betty. I promised your father and I made the same promise to you. I'll never forgive myself that they killed your mum, so don't leave me blaming myself over you. There's only a short window to catch this bastard and I can't waste a minute of it. We need him out of our lives for good. On my own initiative I've narrowed down his location to three. Let's see if we can't do better."

He looked at her intently and moved his head from side to side, like a fighter preparing for the bell. "Look, we can all agree that we need to get set. Let me brief my teams and get them moving. Then we can talk some more."

Martha opened her mouth to keep the argument rolling then thought better of it. When Harry was like this he generally couldn't be budged, so even offering to talk about it was something. She'd just have to wait for the right moment.

Another thought intruded. Harry had said he was talking to former special forces soldiers; she hadn't realised quite how wide his net was cast. She really ought to speak to him about that — but later, much later. For now, she was grateful he was here.

She checked out Krisha, who looked as rumpled as she felt. Martha herself wanted the chance to clean up.

"Harry looks set for a little while. It'll take time to get his teams in place, do you want to grab a shower? I know I would benefit from a wash, and I might have some clean clothes that'll fit you."

"Are you complaining about my body odour?" said Krisha, sniffing her armpit and wrinkling her nose. "On second thought, maybe I do have an issue. If I run, I can make it to mine and back in less than an hour. If you're OK with that."

"Sure I am," said Martha. "If we need to move, we can always meet you there."

"There?"

"If Harry thinks I'm going to stay at arm's length, he's got another think coming. If we can grab Thompson alive, imagine what he might tell us. Bringing him in will be a massive coup and put us in a strong position for the corruption inquiry. But most of all I'd like to look him in the eye and ask him how it feels to be a loser."

"Sounds like a plan to me," said Krisha, getting to her feet and looking around the homely kitchen. She walked out with a quick wave, before coming back.

"How are you going to know you're in the right place? There are three addresses right across London and Harry wants to shoot on sight."

"That's the problem. I'll have to pick the one I think is most likely and then hope for the best." This time Krisha made it out of the door and walked briskly away.

* * *

Four hours later they were in Shepherd Market in the heart of Mayfair, a short walk from Green Park tube station. One of the more expensive parts of London, it boasted a range of pubs, bars, restaurants and coffee shops.

Martha had decided on Shepherd Market as the place on nothing more than a hunch that Thompson would like to be close to one of the older residential parts of London. The two other locations they knew about were brand new developments in Blackfriars and Bankside, both close to the River Thames.

The Mayfair address was a renovated apartment above a wine merchant and close to Ye Grapes public house.

Harry had insisted they keep well back as his team monitored the location. It was a difficult target, but fake police warrant cards had gained his men access to flats opposite, from where they could mount covert surveillance. More than an hour later, the call they had been waiting for came in. "The delivery rider is on his way." It meant the spotters had seen their target.

If Martha and Krisha had been keen to get involved before, now they were practically bouncing, but Harry was having none of it.

"These guys are trained for this. Let them get on with it." He looked rueful. "And we do it your way — if we can. I'm not risking lives if he puts up a fight." After an intense half-hour discussion, Harry had reluctantly agreed not to have Thompson killed on the spot.

"I don't like this. I don't like it at all," he said for the umpteenth time. "If he's dead he can't bother us ever again."

"Just give me a chance to see if he'll talk," was the answer she gave each time. "We really need to know more about what he was up to, especially that mind control. It's the stuff of nightmares."

"This only applies if you're right about him being here. If he's at one of the other two locations, we shoot." To Harry's intense disappointment, the call never came.

Now they were waiting a few hundred yards away as the intrusion squad made their way in. Earlier, they had taken out security cameras over a wide area so were confident they wouldn't be picked out. Working silently to pick the locks, they were soon inside. There was a period of silence before the team leader said, "Target is not here. Repeat not here."

The call provoked consternation.

"He must have seen us and got out in time," said a furious Harry, banging a fist into his other hand. "This area is like a warren."

Martha wanted to look around their enemy's lair, and they made their way inside, pulling on protective gloves. Martha, who had been hoping for some sort of insight into the man, was crushed. The furniture and décor were rental neutral, and he'd left nothing else behind apart from a laptop. She thought that if previous experience was anything to go by, it would be a taunting message and nothing else.

Reluctantly she opened it and stepped back as it flared into life, with a message: *Bad luck, Martha, you should choose your friends more carefully*.

Martha slammed the computer shut but was too late. Looking across at Krisha, she was horrified to see her sweating profusely, despite the cool air. Her heart skipped a beat as she saw that Krisha was holding what looked like a detonator. Martha stared, torn between running away and helping her friend.

"Martha, get out now. I can't hold this much longer."

Martha's stomach lurched and she tried to speak.

"Go! Just go!" shouted Krisha. "You and Harry have got to survive so you can find him and kill him for me." She took a breath, which turned into rapid-fire panting, and her entire body was vibrating with the effort. She looked at Martha, who felt a sudden chill as she realised she would never see her friend's face again. Tears streaming down her face, Krisha grimaced. "I'm sorry, Martha, there's no other way."

"But why are you doing this, Krish? Let us help you, there's no need for this to happen." Martha reached towards her.

"No, Martha, stay back. It has to be this way. He says he will kill every single member of my family unless I do this. He even sends me photos of my kid sister, just to let me know he's always watching. I haven't the slightest doubt he'll make good on his threats. At least this way there's a chance you can get him and take revenge on my part."

A shudder passed through her. "Go, Martha, please. Otherwise it's all a waste. You have to survive."

"Can you give me any clues about Thompson? You must have met him," said Martha.

"I've never met him, but it was Chief Inspector Green who instructed me," she said, tears pouring down her cheeks. "He was waiting outside my flat when I went back earlier. He told me this was the moment I decided if my family lived or died. He even showed me some video of my mum at the supermarket, actually taken inside the supermarket itself. He made sure I saw the timestamp — the footage had only been taken ten minutes before I saw it. I looked into his eyes and felt sick with fear. He didn't care whether any of us lived or died. He was just full of contempt. I cried and he punched me in the stomach, knocking me down. Then he slowly hit me, making sure none of the marks would show. At that moment I knew I was totally powerless.

"I'm so sorry, Martha, he was in total control of me from the moment we first met, but I couldn't tell you, no matter how much I wanted to. Now, for the final time, get out of here. I can't last much longer." She was shaking all over.

Harry broke the spell, lifting Martha off her feet and bundling her through the door. Holding her in a powerful grip, he part ran, part fell down the stairs. As he reached the bottom, she was enveloped by a feeling of immense pressure which hurt her ears. All was weirdly silent for a moment then the world came back to life as the building shook and glass exploded out from the windows. As the space filled with smoke Harry shook her hard.

"Martha, we need to get out of here now." He was covered in dust and looked frightful. She knew she must look the same.

With Harry supporting her, they made their way to the tube station. Being London, no one paid attention to the strange sight. For Martha the journey passed in a blur, and several times she sobbed uncontrollably as she thought of her friend blown to pieces. She'd been angry with Neil

Thompson before, but now she felt part of her heart had turned to ice and would remain that way until Krisha's death was avenged. Right now that only meant one thing. He had to die. There would be no more disagreeing with Harry.

CHAPTER 63

Martha and Harry were back in the kitchen at Dulwich, an open bottle of wine and two full but undrunk glasses on the table between them. For the past two hours, he had listened patiently as she talked and talked, trying to make sense of the disaster. At first she had been determined to confess all, but Harry didn't budge.

"Somehow, she found the strength to save us, even though she knew it would be the last thing she ever did. She didn't do that so you could get thrown out of the police — or even sent to prison."

It was a persuasive argument and one she had reluctantly accepted.

But she was quite incapable of letting everything go.

"Some of this is my fault. If I hadn't given her time to go home she might not have been put in that situation," she said, her eyes brimming over with salty tears and her nose going red from the amount of times she'd blown it. She'd made sure Krisha's family received protection, although it was cold comfort to know they were OK. In some ways it made her sacrifice all the more poignant and added to her furious determination that Green was held to account.

Harry hadn't needed to say anything, just sit there as her words revealed her degree of guilt.

"Why didn't I realise he'd got at her? I should have known. I could have saved her." She stopped talking, feeling suddenly so desperate she worried she might be heading for a breakdown.

"Look at me, Martha," he said urgently. "Really look at me. I know a bit about guilt and how it can break the strongest of us. There are things I've done that I wish I never had, and guilt is the price I pay.

"But you have nothing to be guilty about. You couldn't have known. You never had the slightest worry about Krisha, right until that last moment. You have to find a way to let go of this, not just for your sake, for Betty too. That little girl needs her mum. Her real mum, not this version of you. The only enemy here is Thompson. No one else."

She didn't stop crying, but Harry mentioning Betty had cut through. She'd listened to his words, now she had to trust in her own formidable inner strength to move forward. They sat in silence for a while, then Martha breathed out.

"It seems unfair that questions are going to be asked about what she was up to, and why she was in a flat linked to Neil Thompson." She pounded her fist on the table.

"The only thing I can tell you is that at least no one needs to know how she was trapped by him," said Harry. "That's something."

"It is. And I'll take that secret to my grave," said Martha. She finally reached for her glass of wine.

"To the bravest woman I know." She raised in a toast to her friend. "I wish I'd listened to you, Harry. At least the bastard would be dead now."

Her phone beeped. It was a message from Jonathan Roper:

I've ordered a watch for our friend Tony Green. You and Harry should also know that a police station used as a base by your father — now closed down — was raided a few days ago. The thieves only had one interest. They targeted an old office used by your father and smashed all the walls to pieces. It may be the raiders were searching for something he hid in the wall space. We should meet to discuss once this business with Neil Thompson is concluded.

Martha read it again and then whistled, before wordlessly handing it to Harry.

Harry studied the message then grunted. "How does he know about me?"

"I have no idea," said Martha. "But I'd like to know who raided the police station. My instinct says it wasn't Neil Thompson because he was already focused on us. Why pursue us at the same time. But if not him, then who?"

Harry cracked his knuckles. "I have to admit your dad did have a lot of enemies."

Before Martha could ask him any more questions, her phone beeped again. Jonathan had sent her a picture.

I managed to get them to release that picture to you. I hope it helps.

She opened the attachment. It showed a man in his forties. It was probably her imagination but she thought he looked rather pleased with himself. She showed it to Harry, who stared intently. If you could kill with a look then Harry was doing it.

She reached for her glass of wine again. She took a sip and toasted Krisha, then she gasped.

"Show me that picture again."

Harry held it up.

"They could be brothers."

Harry stared again, then nodded. "Tony Green and Neil Thompson. That would explain a lot. Suppose there is a secret group operating inside the Met. All members of the same family?"

She stared at him.

"I know it sounds crazy," said Harry, throwing his hands in the air. "But there's been rumours that your dad tried to chase down. About a bunch of criminals, all related, who

243

work all over the Met, from the cleaners to the top brass. That would explain what I heard when I was asking around."

"I need to ring Jonathan," said Martha. She had to leave a message since he didn't answer. Half an hour later, they'd just opened a second bottle when Martha's phone rang. She answered and put it on loudspeaker.

"Jonathan Roper here." He spoke quickly and precisely, like a man who valued details.

"I'm so pleased you called. I wanted to—"

Roper cut her off. "Martha, I have bad news. Tony Green has escaped. We tracked him to a private plane to Le Touquet, across the Channel. We know he got off and was picked up by a car. There's no trace of him now."

They talked some more and filled Roper in on the crime family information.

"That fits with our knowledge. If this is true they're very dangerous people. We're going to have to be clever about this."

Martha laughed, but there was no humour in it.

"I intend to get that bastard and make him pay."

THE END

THE JOFFE BOOKS STORY

We began in 2014 when Jasper agreed to publish his mum's much-rejected romance novel and it became a bestseller.

Since then we've grown into the largest independent publisher in the UK. We're extremely proud to publish some of the very best writers in the world, including Joy Ellis, Faith Martin, Caro Ramsay, Helen Forrester, Simon Brett and Robert Goddard. Everyone at Joffe Books loves reading and we never forget that it all begins with the magic of an author telling a story.

We are proud to publish talented first-time authors, as well as established writers whose books we love introducing to a new generation of readers.

We have been shortlisted for Independent Publisher of the Year at the British Book Awards three times, in 2020, 2021 and 2022, and for the Diversity and Inclusivity Award at the Independent Publishing Awards in 2022.

We built this company with your help, and we love to hear from you, so please email us about absolutely anything bookish at feedback@joffebooks.com

If you want to receive free books every Friday and hear about all our new releases, join our mailing list: www.joffebooks.com/contact

And when you tell your friends about us, just remember: it's pronounced Joffe as in coffee or toffee!